DARBY O'GILL AND THE GOOD PEOPLE

DARBY O'GILL
AND THE GOOD PEOPLE

by
Herminie Templeton Kavanagh

ONE FAITHFUL HARP PUBLISHERS
Scranton, Pennsylvania

This book is printed on acid-free paper.

Originally published in the United States of America in 1903 by
McClure, Philips

Slightly revised by the Publisher

Revisions, Editor's Preface, and Introduction © 1998 One Faithful
Harp Publishing Co.

Library of Congress Catalog Card Number 98-067935
ISBN 0-9666701-0-8

One Faithful Harp Publishing Company
P.O. Box 20140
Scranton, PA 18502-0140
717-342-8156

Printed in the United States of America

EDITOR'S PREFACE

Few countries, if any, have been as closely connected to Catholicism as Ireland has. That connection has been the Irish people's glory and their cross. Theirs is a heroic past, which makes it doubly sad to see Ireland going, albeit somewhat reluctantly, the post-Christian way of the rest of the West. But no matter how far the Irish people stray from the Faith, there is always the hope that their rich Catholic past will pull them back.

Herminie Kavanagh's book, *Darby O'Gill and the Good People*, gives us a rare look at an organic Catholic society. Catholicism is in the blood of Kavanagh's characters; they would no sooner question the reality of the Christian God than they would question the reality of the potatoes on the table before them. We, the Catholics of the post-Christian West, need to enter, if only for the few hours that we are with Darby, a world in which the Faith is experienced as an everyday reality and not just as a belief which we hang onto only with an extraordinary effort of the will.

So, welcome to the world of Darby O'Gill. It is not a secular utopia, but a Catholic world—of good whiskey, good people, and grand laughter.

Daniel Neyer
One Faithful Harp Publishing Company

AUTHOR'S PREFACE

This history sets forth the only true account of the adventures of a daring Tipperary man named Darby O'Gill among the Fairies of Sleive-na-mon.

These adventures were first related to me by Mr. Jerry Murtaugh, a reliable car-driver, who goes between Kilcuny and Ballinderg. His own mother is a first cousin of Darby O'Gill.

Herminie T. Kavanagh

INTRODUCTION

There needs to be a word spoken about the fairies, or as they have come to be called, the leprechauns. And as Darby's parish priest, I think I am the one who must say it.

Through my acquaintance with that estimable man, Darby O'Gill, I became personally acquainted with Brian Connors, King of the Fairies. I found him to be a creature trembling under God's judgment and a creature with a distorted admiration for Old Nick, as he calls the devil. But (and this is a crucial 'but') King Brian is not without some redeemable qualities. While not conceding a fraction of an inch to him regarding theology, I will concede him that fraction as regards his personal character.

Which leads me to say that, although Satan and the angels who sided with him are most certainly damned, it *is* possible that King Brian and his fellow fairies, who chose to stay neutral during the war between the good and bad angels, might, at the Last Judgment, make it to heaven, if they are truly repentant. I say this against the opinion of Mr. Jerry Murtaugh, but I thought simple justice and charity demanded that I clear that issue up. Let no reader accuse me of dogmatic universalism, for trying to steer an even-handed Catholic course between rigid Jansenism on the one hand, and universal salvation without the judgment of God on the other.

God bless you all, dear readers. May you take true inspiration from Darby's adventures, and may you all be granted the gift of final perserverance and a safe trip to that Heavenly Emerald Isle at the end of your earthly days.

Father Cassidy
Parish Priest

CONTENTS

ONE

Darby O' Gill and the Good People

Although only one living man of his own free will ever went among them there, still, any well-learned person in Ireland can tell you that the abode of the Good People is in the hollow heart of the great mountain, Sleive-na-mon. That same one man was Darby O'Gill, a cousin of my own mother.

Right and left, generation after generation, the fairies had stolen pigs, young children, old women, young men, cows, churnings of butter from other people, but had never bothered any of our kith or kin until, for some mysterious reason, they soured on Darby, and took the eldest of his three fine pigs.

The next week a second pig went the same way. The third week not a thing had Darby left for the Balinrobe fair. You may easily think how sore and sorry the poor man was, and how Bridget, his wife, and the children carried on. The rent was due, and all left was to sell his cow Rosie to pay it. Rosie was the apple of his eye; he admired and respected the pigs, but he loved Rosie.

Worse luck of all was yet to come. On the morning when Darby went for the cow to bring her into market, bad scrans to the hoof was there; but in her place only a wisp of dirty straw to mock him. Millia murther! What a howling and screeching and cursing did Darby bring back to the house!

Now Darby was a bold man, and a desperate man in his anger as you soon will see. He shoved his feet into a pair of brogues, clapped his hat on his head, and gripped his stick in his hand. "Fairy or no fairy, ghost or goblin, livin' or dead, who took Rosie'll rue the day," he says.

With those wild words he bolted in the direction of Sleive-na-mon.

All day long he climbed like an ant over the hill, looking for hole or cave through which he could get at the prison of Rosie. At times he struck the rocks with his black-thorn, crying out challenge. "Come out, you that took her," he called. "If ye have the courage of a mouse, ye murtherin' thieves, come out!"

No one made answer—at least, not just then. But at night, as he turned, hungry and footsore, toward home, whom should he meet up with on the cross-roads but the old fairy doctor, Sheelah Maguire; well known was she as a spy for the Good People. She spoke up: "Oh, then, you're the foolish, blundherin'-headed man to be saying what you've said, and doing what you've done this day, Darby O'Gill," says she.

"What do I care!" says he, fiercely. "I'd fight the divil for my beautiful cow."

"Then go into Mrs. Hagan's meadow beyant," says Sheelah, "and wait till the moon is up. By an' by ye'll see a herd of cows come down from the mountain, and yer own'll be among them."

"What I'll do then?" asked Darby, his voice trembling with excitement.

"Sorra a hair I care what ye do! But there'll be lads there, and hundreds you won't see, that'll stand no ill words, Darby O'Gill."

"One question more, ma'am," says Darby, as Sheelah was moving away. "How late in the night will they stay without?"

Sheelah caught him by the collar and, pulling his head close, whispered: "When the cock crows the Good People must be safe at home. After cock-crow they have no power to help or to hurt, and every mortal eye can see them plain."

"I thank you kindly," says Darby, "and I bid you good evening, ma'am." He turned away, leaving her standing there alone looking after him; but he was sure he heard voices talking to her and laughing and tittering behind him.

It was dark night when Darby stretched himself on the ground in Hagan's meadow; the yellow rim of the moon just tipped the edge of the hills.

As he lay there in the long grass amidst the silence, there came a cold shudder in the air, and after it had passed the deep cracked voice of a near-by bull-frog called loudly and ballyragging: "The Omadhaun! Omadhaun! Omadhaun!" it said.

From a sloe tree over near the hedge, an owl cried, surprised and trembling: "Who-o-o? who-o-o?" it asked.

At that every frog in the meadow—and there must have been ten thousand of them—took up the answer, and shrieked shrill and high together. "Darby O'Gill! Darby O'Gill! Darby O'Gill!" sang they.

"The Omadhaun! The Omadhaun!" cried the wheezy master frog again. "Who-o? Who-o?" asked the owl. "Darby O'Gill! Darby O'Gill!" screamed the rollicking chorus; and that way they were going over and over again until the bold man was just about to creep off to another spot when, sudden, a hundred slow shadows, stirring up the mists, crept from the mountain way toward him. First he must find if Rosie was among the herd. To creep quiet as a cat through the hedge and reach the first cow was only a minute's work. Then his plan, to wait till cockcrow, with all other sober, sensible thoughts, went clean out of the lad's head before his rage; for cropping eagerly the long, sweet grass, the first beast he met, was Rosie.

With a leap Darby was behind her, his stick falling sharply on her flanks. The ingratitude of that cow almost broke Darby's heart. Rosie turned fiercely on him with a vicious lunge, her two horns aimed at his breast. There was no suppler boy in the parish than Darby, and well for him it was so, for the mad rush the cow gave would have caught any man the least trifle heavy on his legs and ended his days right there. As it was, our hero sprang to one side. As Rosie passed, his left hand gripped her tail. When one of the O'Gills takes hold of a thing he hangs on like a bull-terrier. Away he went, rushing with her.

Now began a race the like of which was never heard of before or since. Ten jumps to the second and a hundred feet to the jump. Rosie's tail standing straight up in the air, firm as an iron bar, and Darby floating straight out behind; a thousand furious fairies flying a short distance after, filling the air with wild commands and threatenings.

Suddenly the sky opened for a crash of lightning that shivered the hills, and a roar of thunder that turned out of their beds every man, woman, and child in four counties. Flash after flash came the lightning, hitting on every side of our hero. If it wasn't for fear of hurting Rosie, the fairies would certainly have killed Darby. As it was, he was stiff with fear, afraid to hold on and afraid to let go, but flew, waving in the air at Rosie's tail like a flag.

As the cow turned into the long, narrow valley which cuts into the east side of the mountain, the Good People caught up with the pair, and what they didn't do to Darby in the line of sticking pins, pulling whiskers, and pinching wouldn't take long to tell. In troth, he was just about to let go his hold and take the chances of a fall when the hillside opened and—whisk! the cow turned into the mountain. Darby found himself flying down a wide, high passage which grew lighter as he went along. He heard the opening behind shut like a trap, and his heart almost stopped beating, for this was the fairies' home in the heart of Sleive-na-mon. He was captured by them!

When Rosie stopped, so stiff were all Darby's joints that he had great trouble loosening himself to come down. He landed among a lot of angry-faced little people, each no higher than your hand, every one wearing a green velvet cloak and a red cap, and in every cap was stuck a white owl's feather.

"We'll take him to the King," says a red-whiskered wee chap. "What he'll do to the murtherin' spalpeen'll be good and plenty!"

With that they marched our bold Darby, a prisoner, down the long passage, which every second grew wider and lighter and fuller of little people.

Sometimes, though, he met with human beings like himself, only the black charm was on them, they having been stolen at some time by the Good People. He saw lost people there from every parish in Ireland, both commoners and gentry. Each was laughing, talking, and diverting himself with another. Off to the sides he could see small cobblers making brogues, tinkers mending pans, tailors sewing cloth, smiths hammering horse-shoes, every one merrily to his trade, making a diversion out of work.

To this day Darby can't tell where the beautiful red light he now saw came from. It was like a soft glow, only it filled the place, making things brighter than day.

Down near the centre of the mountain was a room twenty times higher and broader than the biggest church in the world. As they drew near this room there arose the sound of a reel played on bagpipes. The music was so bewitching that Darby, who was the gracefullest reel-dancer in all Ireland, could hardly make his feet behave themselves.

At the room's edge Darby stopped short and caught his breath, the sight was so entrancing. Set over the broad floor were thousands and thousands of the Good People, facing this way and that, dancing to a reel; while on a throne in the middle of the room sat old Brian Connors, King of the Fairies, blowing on the bagpipes. The little King, with a gold crown on his head, wearing a beautiful green velvet coat and red knee-breeches, sat with his legs crossed, beating time with his foot to the music.

There were many from Darby's own parish; and what was his surprise to see there Maureen McGibney, his own wife's sister, whom he had supposed resting decently in her own grave in holy ground these three years. She had flowers in her brown hair, a fine colour in her cheeks, a gown of white silk and gold, and her green mantle reached to the heels of her pretty red slippers.

There she was gliding back and forth, ferninst a little gray-whiskered, round-stomached fairy man, as though there was never a care nor a sorrow in the world.

As I told you before, I tell you again, Darby was the finest reel-dancer in all Ireland; and he came from a family of dancers, though I say it who shouldn't, as he was my mother's own cousin. Three things in the world banish sorrow—love and whisky and music. So, when the surprise of it all melted a little, Darby's feet led him in to the thick of the throng, right under the throne of the King, where he flung care to the winds and put his heart and mind into his two nimble feet. Darby's dancing was such that pretty soon those around stood still to admire.

There's a saying come down in our family through generations which I still hold to be true, that the better the music the easier the step. Sure never did mortal men dance to so fine a tune, and never so supple a dancer did such a tune meet up with.

Fair and graceful he began. Backward and forward, side-step and turn; cross over, then forward; a hand on his hip and his stick twirling free; side-step and forward; cross over again; bow to his partner, and hammer the floor.

It wasn't long till half the dancers crowded around, admiring, clapping their hands, and shouting encouragement. The old King grew so excited that he laid down the pipes, took up his fiddle, came down from the throne, and standing ferninst Darby, began a finer tune than the first.

The dancing lasted a whole hour, no one speaking a word except to cry out, "Foot it, ye divil!", "Aisy now, he's threading on flowers!", and, "Hooroo! hooroo! hooray!" Then the King stopped and said: "Well, that bates Banagher, and Banagher bates the worruld! Who are you and how came you here?"

Then Darby up and told the whole story.

When he had finished, the King looked serious. "I'm glad you came, an' I'm sorry you came," he says. "If we had put our charm on you outside to bring you in you'd never die till the ind of the worruld. Those willing to come with us can't come at all, at all; and here you are of your own free act and will. Howsomever, you're here, and we daren't let you go outside to tell others of what you have seen, and so give us a bad name about—about taking things, you know. We'll make you as comfortable as we can; and so you won't worry about Bridget and the childher, I'll have a goold sovereign left with them every day of their lives. But I wish we had comeither on you," he says with a sigh, "for it's aisy to see you're great company. Now, come up to my place and have a noggin of punch for friendship's sake," says he.

That's how Darby O'Gill began his six months' stay with the Good People. Not a thing was left undone to make Darby contented and happy. A civiller people than the Good People he never met. At first he couldn't get over saying, "God save all here," and "God save you kindly," and things like that, which was like burning them with a hot iron.

If it weren't for Maureen McGibney, Darby would be in Sleive-na-mon at this hour. Sure she was always the wise girl, ready with her crafty plans and warnings. On a day when they two were sitting alone together she says to him: "Darby, dear," says she, "it isn't right for a dacint man of family to be spending his days cavortin' and idlin' and fillin' the hours with sport and nonsense. We must get you out of here; for what is a sovereign a day to compare with the care and protection of a father?" she says.

"Thrue for ye!" moaned Darby, "and my heart is just splittin' for a sight of Bridget an' the childher. Bad luck to the day I set so much store on a dirty, ongrateful, treacherous cow!"

"I know well how you feel," says Maureen, "for I'd give the world to say three words to Bob Broderick, that ye tell me that out of grief for me he has never kept company with any other girl till this day. But that'll never be," she says, "because I must stop here till the Day of Judgment," says she, beginning to cry. "But if you get out, you'll bear a message to Bob for me, maybe?" she says.

"It's aisy to talk about going out, but how can it be done?" asked Darby.

"There's a way," says Maureen, wiping her big, gray eyes, "but it may take years. First, you must know that the Good People can never put their charm on anyone who is willing to come with them. That's whay you came safe. Then, agin, they can't work harm in the daylight, and after cock-crow any mortal eye can see them plain; nor can they harm anyone who has a sprig of holly, nor pass over a leaf or twig of holly, because that's Christmas bloom. Well, there's a certain word for a charm that opens the side of the mountain, and I will try to find it out for you. Without that word all the armies in the worruld couldn't get out or in. But you must be patient and wise and wait."

"I will so, with the help of God," says Darby.

The next night she came to Darby again. "Watch yerself now," she says, "for to-night they're going to lave the door of the mountain open to thry you; and if you stir two steps outside they'll put the comeither on you," she says.

Sure enough, when Darby took his walk down the passage after supper, as he did every night, there the side of the mountain lay wide open and no one in sight. The temptation to make one rush was great; but he only looked out a minute, and went whistling down the passage, knowing well that a hundred hidden eyes were on him the while. For a dozen nights after it was the same.

At another time Maureen said: "The King himself is going to thry you hard the day, so beware!" She had no sooner said the words than Darby was called for, and went up to the King.

"Darby, my sowl," says the King, in a soothering way, "have this noggin of punch. A betther never was brewed; it's the last we'll have for many a day. I'm going to set you free, Darby O'Gill, that's what I am."

"Why, King," says Darby, putting on a mournful face, "how have I offended ye?"

"No offence at all," says the King, "only we're depriving you."

"No depravity in life!" says Darby. "I have lashins and lavings to ate and to drink and nothing but fun an' divarsion all day long. Out in the worruld it was nothing but work and throuble and sickness, disappointment and care."

"But Bridget and the childher?" says the King, giving him a sharp look out of half-shut eyes.

"Oh, as for that, King," says Darby, "it's aisier for a widow to get a husband or for orphans to find a father than it is for them to pick up a sovereign a day."

The King looked mighty satisfied and smoked for a while without a word.

"Would you mind goin' out an evenin' now and then, helpin' the boys to mind the cows?" he asked at last.

Darby feared to trust himself outside in their company.

"Well, I'll tell ye how it is," replied my brave Darby. "Some of the neighbours might see me, and spread the report on me that I'm with the fairies and that'd disgrace Bridget and the childher," he says.

The King knocked ashes from his pipe.

"You're a wise man, besides being the hoight of good company," says he, "and it's sorry I am you didn't take my word, for then we would have you always, at laste till the Day of Judgement, when—but that's nayther here nor there! Howsomever, we'll bother you about it no more."

From that day they treated him as one of their own.

It was nearly five months after that Maureen plucked Darby by the coat and led him off to a lonely spot. "I've got the word," she says.

"Have you, faith! What is it?" says Darby, all of a tremble.

Then she whispered the word.

Three hours after this, my bold Darby was sitting at his own fireside talking to Bridget and the children. The neighbours were hurrying to him down every road and through every field, carrying armfuls of holly bushes, as he had sent word for them to do. He knew well he'd have fierce and savage visitors before morning.

After they had come with the holly, he had them make a circle of it so thick around the house that a fly couldn't walk through without touching a twig or leaf. But that was not all.

You'll know what a wise girl and what a crafty girl that Maureen was when you hear what the neighbours did next. They made a second ring of holly outside the first, so that the house sat in two great wreaths, one wreath around the other. The outside ring was much the bigger, and left a good space between it and the first, with room for ever so many people to stand there. It was like the inner ring, except for a little gate, left open as though by accident, where the fairies could walk in.

But it wasn't an accident at all, only the wise plan of Maureen's; for nearby this little gap, in the outside wreath, lay a sprig of holly with a bit of twine tied to it. Then the twine ran along up to Darby's house, and in through the window, where its end lay convenient to his hand. A little pull on the twine would drag the stray piece of holly into the gap and close tight the outside ring.

It was a trap, you see. When the fairies walked in through the gap the twine was to be pulled, and so they were to be made prisoners between the two rings of holly. They couldn't get into Darby's house because the circle of holly nearest the house was so tight that a fly couldn't get through without touching the blessed tree or its wood. Likewise, when the gap in the outer wreath was closed, they couldn't get out again. Well, anyway, these things were hardly finished and fixed when the dusky brown of the hills warned the neighbours of twilight, and they scurried like frightened rabbits to their homes.

Only one amongst them all had courage to sit inside Darby's house waiting the dreadful visitors, and that one was Bob Broderick. What vengeance was in store couldn't be guessed at all, at all, only it was sure to be more terrible than any yet wreaked on mortal man.

Not in Darby's house alone was the terror, for in their anger the Good People might lay waste the whole parish. The roads and fields were empty and silent in the darkness. Not a window glimmered with light for miles around. Many a blackguard who hadn't said a prayer for years was down on his marrow bones among the decent members of his family, thumping his craw and roaring his Pater and Aves.

In Darby's quiet house, against which the cunning, the power, and the fury of the Good People would first break, you can't think of half the suffering of Bridget and the children, as they lay huddled together on the settle-bed; nor of the strain on Bob and Darby, who sat smoking their dudeens and whispering anxiously together.

For some reason or other the Good People were long in coming. Ten o'clock struck, then eleven, after that twelve, and not a sound from the outside. The silence, and then no sign of any kind, had them all just about crazy, when suddenly there fell a sharp rap on the door.

"Millia murther," whispered Darby, "we're in for it. They've crossed the two rings of holly and are at the door itself."

The children begun to cry, and Bridget said her prayers out loud; but no one answered the knock.

"Rap, rap, rap," on the door, then a pause.

"God save all here!" cried a queer voice from the outside.

Now no fairy would say "God save all here," so Darby took heart and opened the door. Who should be standing there but Sheelah Maguire, a spy for the Good People. So angry were Darby and Bob that they snatched her within the threshold, and before she knew it they had her tied hand and foot, wound a cloth around her mouth, and rolled her under the bed. Within the minute a thousand rustling voices sprung from outside. Through the window, in the clear moonlight, Darby marked weeds and grass being trampled by invisible feet beyond the farthest ring of holly.

Suddenly broke a great cry. The gap in the first ring was found. Signs were plainly seen of uncountable feet rushing through and spreading about the nearer wreath. After that a howl of madness from the little men and women; Darby had pulled his twine and the trap was closed, with five thousand of the Good People entirely at his mercy.

Princes, princesses, dukes, dukesses, earls, earlesses, and all the quality of Sleive-na-mon were prisoners. Not more than a dozen of the last to come escaped, and they flew back to tell the King.

For an hour they raged. All the bad names ever called to mortal man were given free, but Darby said never a word. "Pickpocket!", "Sheep-stayler!", "Murtherin' thafe of a blaggard!" were the softest words thrown at him.

By and by, howsomever, as it began to grow near to cockcrow, their talk grew a great deal civiller. Then came begging, pleading, promising, and entreating, but the doors of the house still stayed shut and its windows down.

Pretty soon Darby's old rooster, Terry, came down from his perch, yawned, and flapped his wings a few times. At that the terror and the screeching of the Good People would have melted the heart of a stone.

All of a sudden a fine clear voice rose from beyond the crowd. The King had come. The other fairies grew still listening.

"Ye murtherin' thafe of the worruld," says the King, grandly, "what are ye doin' wid my people?"

"Keep a civil tongue in yer head, Brian Connors," says Darby, sticking his head out the window, "for I'm as good a man as you, any day," says Darby.

At that minute Terry, the cock, flapped his wings and crowed. In a flash there sprang into full view the crowd of Good People—dukes, earls, princes, quality and commoners, with their ladies—jammed thick together about the house; every one of them with his head thrown back bawling and crying, and tears as big as pigeon-eggs rolling down their cheeks.

A few feet away, on a straw-pile in the barnyard, stood the King, his gold crown tilted on the side of his head, his long green cloak about him and his rod in his hand, but trembling all over.

In the middle of the crowd, but towering high above them all, stood Maureen McGibney in her cloak of green and gold, her pretty brown hair falling down her shoulders, and she—the crafty villain—crying and bawling and abusing Darby with the best of them.

"What'll you have an' let them go?" says the King.

"First an' foremost," says Darby, "take yer spell off that slip of a girl there, an' send her into the house."

In a second Maureen was standing inside the door, her both arms about Bob's neck and her head on his collar-bone.

What they said to each other, and what they done in the way of embracing and kissing and crying I won't take time in telling you.

"Next," says Darby, "send back Rosie and the pigs."

"I expected that," says the King. And at those words they saw a black bunch coming through the air, and in a few seconds Rosie and the three pigs walked into the stable.

"Now," says Darby, "promise in the name of Ould Nick" ('tis by him the Good People swear) "never to moil nor meddle again with anyone or anything from this parish."

The King was fair put out by this. Howsomever, he said at last: "You ongrateful scoundrel, in the name of Ould Nick I promise."

"So far, so good," says Darby: "but the worst is yet to come. Now you must raylase from your spell every sowl you've stole from this parish; and besides, you must send me two hundhred pounds in goold."

Well, the King gave a roar of anger that was heard in the next barony.

"Ye high-handed, hard-hearted robber," he says, "I'll never consent!" says he.

"Plase yeself," says Darby. "I see Father Cassidy comin' down the hedge," he says, "an' he has a prayer for ye all in his book that'll burn ye up like wisps of sthraw if he ever catches ye here," says Darby.

With that the roaring and bawling was pitiful to hear, and in a few minutes a bag with two hundred gold sovereigns in it was thrown at Darby's threshold; and fifty people, young and some of them old, flew over and stood beside the King. Some of them had spent years with the fairies. Their relatives thought them dead and buried. They were the lost ones from that parish.

With that Darby pulled the bit of twine again, opening the trap, and it wasn't long until every fairy was gone.

The green coat of the last one was hardly out of sight when, sure enough, who should come up but Father Cassidy, his book in his hand. He looked at the fifty people who had been with the fairies standing there—the poor creatures—trembling and wondering and afeared to go their homes.

Darby told him what had happened.

"Ye foolish man," says the priest, "you could have got out every poor presoner that's locked in Sleive-na-mon, let alone those from this parish."

One could have scraped with a knife the surprise off Darby's face.

"Would yer Reverence have me let out the Corkonians, the Connaught men, and the Fardowns, I ask ye?" he says, hotly. "When Mrs. Malowney there goes home and finds that Tim has married the Widow Hogan, ye'll say I let out too many, even of this parish, I'm thinkin'."

"But," says the priest, "ye might have got two hundhred pounds for aich of us."

"If aich had two hundhred pounds, what comfort would I have in being rich?" asked Darby again. "To enjoy well being rich there should be plenty of poor," says Darby.

"God forgive ye, ye selfish man!" says Father Cassidy.

"There's another rayson besides," says Darby. "I never got betther nor friendlier thratement than I had from the Good People. An' the divil a hair of their heads I'd hurt more than need be," he says.

Some way or other the King heard of this saying, and was so mightily pleased that the next night a jug of the finest poteen was left at Darby's door.

After that, indeed, many's the winter night, when the snow lay so heavy that no neighbour was stirring, and when Bridget and the children were in bed, Darby sat by the fire, a noggin of hot punch in his hand, arguing and getting news of the whole world. A little man with a gold crown on his head, a green cloak on his back, and one foot thrown over the other, sat ferninst him by the hearth.

TWO

Darby O'Gill and the Leprechaun

The news that Darby O'Gill had spent six months with the Good People spread fast and far and wide.

At fair or hurling or market he would be backed by a crowd against some convenient wall, and there for hours men, women, and children, with jaws dropping and eyes bulging, would stand ferninst him listening to half-frightened questions or to bold, mysterious answers.

Always, though, one bit of advice ended his discourse: "Nayther make nor moil nor meddle with the fairies," Darby'd say. "If you're going along the lonely boreen at night and you hear, from some fairy fort, a sound of fiddles, or of piping, or of sweet woices singing, or of little feet patthering in the dance, don't turn your head, but say your prayers an' hould on your way. The pleasures the Good People'll share with you have a sore sorrow hid in them, an' the gifts they'll offer are only made to break hearts with."

Things went this a-way till one day in the market, over among the cows, Maurteen Cavanaugh, the schoolmaster—a cross-faced, argufying old man he was—contradicted Darby point-blank. "Stay a bit," says Maurteen, catching Darby by the coat-collar. "You forget about the little fairy cobbler, the Leprechaun," he says. "You can't deny that to catch the Leprechaun is great luck entirely. If one only fix the glance of his eye on the cobbler, that look makes the fairy a presoner—

one can do anything with him as long as a human look covers the little lad—and he'll give the favours of three wishes to buy his freedom," says Maurteen.

At that Darby, smiling high and knowledgeable, made answer over the heads of the crowd.

"God help your sinse, honest man!" he says. "Around the favours of thim same three wishes is a bag of thricks an' cajolories and conditions that'll defayt the wisest.

"First of all, if the look be taken from the little cobbler for as much as the wink of an eye, he's gone forever," he says. "Man alive, even when he does grant the favours of the three wishes, you're not safe, for, if you tell anyone you've seen the Leprechaun, the favours melt like snow, or if you make a fourth wish that day—whiff! they turn to smoke. Take my adwice—nayther make nor moil nor meddle with the fairies."

"Thrue for ye," spoke up long Pether McCarthy, siding in with Darby. "Didn't Barney McBride, on his way to early mass one May morning, catch the fairy cobbler sewing an' workin' away under a hedge. 'Have a pinch of snuff, Barney agra,' says the Leprechaun, handing up the little snuff-box. But, mind ye, when my poor Barney bint to take a thumb an' finger full, what did the little villain do but fling the box, snuff and all, into Barney's face. An' thin, whilst the poor lad was winkin' and blinkin', the Leprechaun gave one leap and was lost in the reeds.

"Thin, again, there was Peggy O'Rourke, who captured him fair an' square in a hawthorn-bush. In spite of his wiles she wrung from him the favours of the three wishes. Knowing, of course, that if she towld of what had happened to her the spell was broken and the wishes wouldn't come thrue, she hurried home, aching and longing to in some way find from her husband Andy what wishes she'd make.

"Throwing open her own door, she said, 'What would ye wish for most in the world, Andy dear? Tell me an' your wish'll come thrue,' says she. A peddler was crying his wares out in the lane. 'Lanterns, tin lanterns!' cried the peddler. 'I wish I had one of thim lanterns,' says Andy, careless, and bendin' over to get a coal for his pipe, when, lo and behold, there was the lantern in his hand.

"Well, so vexed was Peggy that one of her fine wishes should be wasted on a palthry tin lantern, that she lost all patience with him. 'Why thin, bad scran to you!' says she—not mindin' her own words—'I wish the lantern was fastened to the ind of your nose!'

"The word wasn't well out of her mouth till the lantern was hung swinging from the ind of Andy's nose in a way that the wit of man couldn't loosen. It took the third and last of Peggy's wishes to relayse Andy."

"Look at that, now!" cried a dozen voices from the admiring crowd. "Darby said so from the first."

Well, after a time people used to come from miles around to see Darby and sit under the straw-stack beside the stable to advise with our hero about their most important business—what was the best time for the setting of hens, or what was good to cure colic in children, and things like that.

Any man so persecuted with admiration and heroification might easily feel his chest swell out a bit, so it's no wonder that Darby set himself up for a knowledgeable man.

He took to talking slow and shutting one eye when he listened, and he walked with a knowledgeable twist to his shoulders. He grew monstrously fond of fairs and public gatherings where people made much of him, and he lost every ounce of liking he ever had for hard work.

Things went on with him in this way from bad to worse, and where it would have ended no man knows, if one unlucky morning he hadn't refused to bring in a creel of turf his wife Bridget had asked him to fetch her. The unfortunate man said it was no work for the likes of him.

The last word was still on Darby's lips when he realised his mistake, and he'd have given the world to have the saying back again.

For a minute you could have heard a pin drop. Bridget, instead of being in a hurry to begin at him, was cruel deliberate. She planted herself in the door, her two fists on her hips, and her lips shut.

The look Julius Sayser'd throw at a servant-girl he'd caught stealing sugar from the royal cupboard was the glance she waved up and down from Darby's toes to his head, and from his head to his brogues again.

Then she began and talked steady as a fall of hail that has now and then a bit of lightning and thunder mixed in it.

The knowledgeable man stood pretending to brush his hat and trying to look brave, but the heart inside of him was melting like butter.

Bridget began easily by carelessly mentioning a few of Darby's best known weaknesses. After that she took up some of them not so well known, being ones Darby himself had serious doubts about having at all. But on these last she was more severe than on the first. Through it all he daren't say a word—he only smiled lofty and bitter.

'Twas but natural next for Bridget to explain what a poor creature her husband was the day she got him, and what she might have been if she had married either one of the six others who had asked her. The step for her was a little one, then, to the shortcomings and misfortunes of his blood relations, which she followed back to the blackguardisms of his fourth cousin, Phelim McFadden.

Even in his misery poor Darby couldn't but marvel at her wonderful memory.

By the time she began talking of her own family, and especially about her Aunt Honoria O'Shaughnessy, who had once shook hands with a Bishop, and who in the rebellion of '98 had thrown a brick at a Lord Liftenant when he was riding by, Darby was as wilted and as forlorn-looking as a rooster caught out in the winter rain.

He lost more pride in those few minutes than it had taken months to gather and hoard. It kept falling in great drops from his forehead.

Just as Bridget was leading up to what Father Cassidy calls a "pur-roar-ration"—that being the part of your wife's discourse when, after telling you all she's done for you, and all she's stood from your relations, she breaks down and cries, and so smothers you entirely—just as she was coming to that, I say, Darby scrooged his caubeen down on his head, stuck his fingers in his two ears, and, making one grand rush through the door, bolted as fast as his legs could carry him down the road toward Sleive-na-mon Mountains.

Bridget stood on the step looking after him, too surprised for a word. With his fingers still in his ears, so that he couldn't hear her commands to turn back, he ran without stopping till he came to the willow-tree near Joey Hooligan's forge. There he slowed down to fill his lungs with the fresh, sweet air.

'Twas one of those warm-hearted, laughing autumn days which steals for a while the bonnet and shawl of the May. The sun, from a sky of feathery whiteness, leaned over, telling jokes to the world, and the gold harvest-fields and purple hills, lazy and contented, laughed back at the sun. Even the blackbird flying over the haw-tree looked down and sang to those below, "God save all here," and the linnet from her bough answered back quick and sweet, "God save you kindly, sir!"

With such pleasant sights and sounds and twitterings at every side, our hero didn't feel the time passing till he was on top of the first hill of the Sleive-na-mon Mountains, which, as everyone knows, is called the Pig's Head.

It wasn't quite lonesome enough on the Pig's Head, so our hero plunged into the valley and climbed the second mountain—the Divil's Pillow—where 'twas lonesome and deserted enough to suit anyone.

Beneath the shade of a tree, for the day was warm, he sat himself down in the long, sweet grass, lit his pipe, and let his mind go free. But, as he did, his thoughts rose together like a flock of frightened, angry pheasants, and whirred back to the audacious things Bridget had said about his relations.

Wasn't she the mendacious, humbrageous woman, he thought, to say such things about as elegant stock as the O'Gills and the O'Gradys?

Why, Wullum O'Gill, Darby's uncle, at that minute, was head butler at Castle Brophy, and was known far and wide as being one of the finest scholars and as having the most beautiful pair of legs in all Ireland!

This same Wullum O'Gill had told Bridget in Darby's own hearing, on a day when the three were going through the great picture-gallery at Castle Brophy, that the O'Gills at one time had been Kings in Ireland.

Darby never since could remember whether this time was before the flood or after the flood. Bridget said it was during the flood, but surely that saying was nonsense.

Howsomever, Darby knew his Uncle Wullum was right, for he often felt in himself the signs of greatness. And now as he sat alone on the grass he said out loud: "If I had me rights I'd be doing nothing all day long but sittin' on a throne, an' playin' games of forty-five with the Lord Liftenant an' some of me generals. There never was a lord that likes good ating or dhrinking betther nor I, or who hates worse to get up airly in the morning. That last disloike I'm tould is a great sign entirely of gentle blood the worruld over," says he.

As for the wife's people, the O'Hagans and the O'Shaughnessys, well—they were no great shakes, he said to himself, at least so far as looks were concerned. All the handsomeness in Darby's children came from his own side of the family. Even Father Cassidy said the children took after the O'Gills.

"If I were rich," said Darby, to a lazy old bumble-bee who was droning and tumbling in front of him, "I'd have a castle like Castle Brophy, with a great picture-gallery in it. On one wall I'd put the picture of the O'Gills and the O'Gradys, and on the wall ferninst them I'd have the O'Hagans an' the O'Shaughnessys."

At that idea his heart bubbled in a new and fierce delight. "Bridget's people," he says again, scowling at the bee, "would look four times as common as they rayly are, whin they were compared in that way with my own relations. An' whenever Bridget got rampageous I'd take her in and show her the difference betwixt the two clans, just to punish her, so I would."

How long the lad sat that way warming the cold thoughts of his heart with drowsy, pleasant dreams and misty longings he don't rightly know, when—tack, tack, tack, tack, came the busy sound of a little hammer from the other side of a fallen oak.

"Be jingo!" he says to himself with a start, "'tis the Leprechaun that's in it."

In a second he was on his hands and knees, the tails of his coat flung across his back, and he crawling softly toward the sound of the hammer. Quiet as a mouse he lifted himself up on the mossy log to look over, and there before his two popping eyes was a sight of wonderation.

Sitting on a white stone and working away like fury, hammering pegs into a little red shoe, half the size of your thumb, was a bald-headed old cobbler of about twice the height of your hand. On the top of a round, snub nose was perched a pair of horn-rimmed spectacles, and a narrow fringe of iron-gray whiskers grew under his stubby chin. The brown leather apron he wore was so long that it covered his green knee-breeches and almost hid the knitted gray stockings.

The Leprechaun—for it was he indeed—as he worked, mumbled and muttered in great discontent: "Oh, haven't I the hard, hard luck," he said. "I'll never have thim done in time for her to dance in tonight. So, thin, I'll be kilt entirely," says he. "Was there ever another quane of the fairies as wearing on shoes an' brogues an' dancin'-slippers? Haven't I the—" Looking up, he saw Darby.

"The top of the day to you, dacint man!" says the cobbler, jumping up. Giving a sharp cry, he pointed quick at Darby's stomach. "But, wirra, wirra, what's that wooly, ugly thing you have crawling an' creepin' on your weskit?" he said, pretending to be all excited.

"Sorra thing on my weskit," answered Darby, cool as ice, "or anywhere else that'll make me take my two bright eyes off'n you—not for a second," says he.

"Well! Well! Will you look at that, now?" laughed the cobbler. "Mark how quick an' handy he took me up! Will you have a pinch of snuff, clever man?" he asked, holding up the little box.

"Is it the same snuff you gave Barney McBride a while ago?" asked Darby, sarcastic. "Lave off your foolishness," says our hero, growing fierce, "and grant me at once the favours of the three wishes, or I'll have you smoking like a herring in my own chimney before nightfall," says he.

At that the Leprechaun, seeing that he but wasted time on so knowledgeable a man as Darby O'Gill, surrendered, and granted the favours of the three wishes. "What is it you ask?" says the cobbler, himself turning, on a sudden, very sour and sullen.

"First an' foremost," says Darby, "I want a home of my ansisthers, an' it must be a castle like Castle Brophy, with pictures of my kith an' kin on the wall, and then facing them, pictures of my wife Bridget's kith an' kin on the other wall."

"That favour I give ye, that wish I grant ye," says the fairy, making the shape of a castle on the ground with his awl. "What next?" he grunted.

"I want goold enough for me an' my generations to enjoy in grandeur the place forever."

"Always the goold," sneered the little man, bending to draw with his awl on the turf the shape of a purse. "Now for your third and last wish. Have a care!"

"I want the castle set on this hill—the Divil's Pillow— where we two stand," says Darby. Then sweeping with his arm, he says, "I want the land about to be my demesne."

The Leprechaun stuck his awl on the ground. "That wish I give you, that wish I grant you," he says. With that he straightened himself up, and grinning most aggravating the while, he looked Darby over from top to toe. "You're a foine, knowledgeable man, but have a care of the fourth wish!" says he.

Because there was more of a challenge than friendly warning in what the small lad said, Darby snapped his fingers at him and cried: "Have no fear, little man! If I got all Ireland ground for making a fourth wish, however small, before midnight I'd not make it. I'm going home now to fetch Bridget an' the childher, and the only fear or unaisiness I have is that you'll not keep your word, so as to have the castle ready before us when I come back."

"Oho! I'm not to be thrusted, amn't I?" screeched the little lad, flaring into a blazing passion. He jumped upon the log that was betwixt them, and with one fist behind his back shook the other at Darby. "You ignorant, auspicious-minded blaggard!" says he. "How dare the likes of you say the likes of that to the likes of me!" cried the cobbler. "I'd have you to know," he says, "that I had a repitation for truth an' voracity ayquil if not shuperior to the best, before you were born!" he shouted. "I'll take no high talk from a man that's afraid to give words to his own wife whin she's in a tantrum!" says the Leprechaun.

"It's aisy to know you're not a married man," says Darby, mighty scornful, "bekase if you—"

The lad stopped short, forgetting what he was going to say in his surprise and agitation, for the far side of the mountain was waving up and down before his eyes like a great green blanket that is being shook by two women, while at the same time high spots of turf on the hillside toppled sidewise to level themselves up with the low places. The enchantment had already begun to make things ready for the castle. A dozen fine trees that stood in a little grove bent their heads quickly together, and then by some invisible hand they were plucked up by the roots and dropped aside much the same as a man might grasp a handful of weeds and fling them from his garden.

The ground under the knowledgeable man's feet began to rumble and heave. He waited for no more. With a cry that was half of gladness and half of fear, he turned on his heel and started on a run down into the valley, leaving the little cobbler standing on the log, shouting abuse after him and ballyragging him as he ran.

So excited was Darby that, going up the Pig's Head, he was nearly run over by a crowd of great brown building stones which were moving down slow and orderly like a flock of driven sheep,—but they moved without so much as bruising a blade of grass or bending a twig, as they came.

Only once, and that at the top of the Pig's Head, he threw a look back.

The Divil's Pillow was in a great commotion; a whirlwind was sweeping over it—whether of dust or of mist he couldn't tell.

After this, Darby never looked back again or to the right or the left of him, but kept straight on till he found himself, panting and puffing, at his own kitchen door. 'Twas ten minutes before he could speak, but at last, when he told Bridget to make ready herself and the children to go up to the Divil's Pillow with him, for once in her life that remarkable woman, without asking, How comes it so, What reason have you, or Why should I do it, set to work washing the children's faces.

Maybe she dabbed a little more soap in their eyes than was needful, for 'twas a habit she had; though this time if she did, not a whimper broke from the little heroes. For the matter of that, not one word, good, bad or indifferent, did herself speak till the whole family were trudging down the lane two by two, marching like soldiers.

As they came near the first hill along its sides the evening twilight turned from purple to brown, and at the top of the Pig's Head the darkness of a black night swooped suddenly down on them. Darby hurried on a step or two ahead, and resting his hand upon the large rock that crowns the hill, looked anxiously over to the Divil's Pillow. Although he was ready for something fine, yet the greatness of the fineness that met his gaze knocked the breath out of him.

Across the deep valley, and on top of the second mountain, he saw lined against the evening sky the roof of an immense castle, with towers and parapets and battlements. Under the towers a thousand sullen windows glowed red in the black walls. Castle Brophy couldn't hold a candle to it.

"Behold!" says Darby, flinging out his arm, and turning to his wife, who had just come up—"behold the castle of my ansisthers who were my forefathers!"

"How," says Bridget, quick and scornful—"how could your aunt's sisters be your four fathers?"

What Darby was going to say to her he don't just remember, for at that instant from the right-hand side of the mountain came a cracking of whips, a rattling of wheels, and the rush of horses, and lo and behold! a great dark coach with flashing lamps, and drawn by four coal-black horses, dashed up the hill and stopped beside them. Two shadowy men were on the driver's box.

"Is this Lord Darby O'Gill?" asked one of them, in a deep muffled voice. Before Darby could reply Bridget took the words out of his mouth.

"It is!" she cried, in a kind of a half cheer, "an' Lady O'Gill an' the childher."

"Then hurry up!" says the coachman. "Your supper's gettin' cowld."

Without waiting for anyone Bridget flung open the carriage-door, and pushing Darby aside jumped in among the cushions. Darby, his heart sizzling with vexation at her audaciousness, lifted in one after another the children, and then got in himself.

He couldn't understand at all the change in his wife, for she had always been the orderliest, most modest woman in the parish.

Well, he'd no sooner shut the door than crack went the whip, the horses gave a spring, the carriage jumped, and down the hill they went. For fastness there was never another carriage-ride like that before nor since. Darby held tight with both hands to the window, his face pressed against the glass. He couldn't tell whether the horses were only flying or whether the coach was falling down the hill into the valley. By the hollow feeling in his stomach he thought they were falling. He was striving to think of some prayers when there came a terrible jolt which sent his two heels against the roof and his head betwixt the cushions. As he righted himself the wheels began to grate on a gravelled road, and plainly they were dashing up the side of the second mountain.

Even so, they couldn't have gone far when the carriage drew up in a flurry, and he saw through the gloom a high iron gate being slowly opened.

"Pass on," said a voice from somewhere in the shadows; "their supper's getting cowld."

As they flew under the great archway Darby had a glimpse of the thing which had opened the gate, and had said their supper was getting cold. It was standing on its hind legs—in the darkness he couldn't be quite sure as to its shape, but it was either a Bear or a Lion.

His mind was in a ponder about this when, with a swirl and a bump, the carriage stopped another time, and now it stood before a broad flight of stone steps which led up to the main door of the castle. Darby, half afraid, peering out through the darkness, saw a square of light high above him which came from the open hall door. Three servants in livery stood waiting on the threshold.

"Make haste, make haste!" says one, in a doleful voice; "their supper's gettin' cowld."

Hearing these words, Bridget immediately bounced out, and was half-way up the steps before Darby could catch her and hold her till the children came up.

"I never in all my life saw her so audacious," he says, half crying, and linking her arm to keep her back, and then, with the children following two by two, according to size, the whole family paraded up the steps, till Darby, with a gasp of delight, stopped on the threshold of a splendid hall. From a high ceiling hung great flags from every nation and domination, which swung and swayed in the dazzling light.

Two lines of men and maid servants dressed in silks and satins and brocades, stood facing each other, bowing and smiling and waving their hands in welcome. The two lines stretched down to the gold stairway at the far end of the hall.

For half of one minute Darby, every eye in his head as big as a tea-cup, stood hesitating. Then he said, "Why should it flutther me? Arrah, ain't it all mine? Aren't all these people in me pay? I'll engage it's a pritty penny all this grandeur is costing me to keep up this minute." He threw out his chest. "Come on, Bridget!" he says; "let's go into the home of my ansisthers."

Howandever, scarcely had he stepped into the beautiful place when two pipers with their pipes, two fiddlers with their fiddles, two flute-players with their flutes, and they dressed in scarlet and gold, stepped out in front of him, and thus to melodious music the family proudly marched down the hall, climbed up the golden stairway at its end, and then turned to enter the biggest room Darby had ever seen.

Something in his soul whispered that this was the picture-gallery.

"Be the powers of Pether!" says the knowledgeable man to himself, "I wouldn't be in Bridget's place this minute for a hatful of money! Wait, oh just wait, till she has to compare her own relations with my own foine people! I know how she'll feel, but I wondher what she'll say," he says.

The thought that all the unjust things, all the unreasonable things Bridget had said about his kith and kin were just going to be disproved and turned against herself, made him proud and almost happy.

But wirrastrue! He should have remembered his own advice not to make nor moil nor meddle with the fairies, for here he was to get the first hard welt from the little Leprechaun.

It was the picture-gallery sure enough, but how terribly different everything was from what the poor lad expected. There on the left wall, grand and noble, shone the pictures of Bridget's people. Of all the well-dressed, handsome, proud-appearing persons in the whole world, the O'Hagans and the O'Shaughnessys would compare with the best. This was a hard enough crack, though a more crushing knock was to come. Ferninst them on the right wall glowered the O'Gills and the O'Gradys, and of all the ragged, sheep-stealing, hangdog-looking villains one ever saw in jail or out of jail, it was Darby's kindred.

The place of honour on the right wall was given to Darby's fourth cousin, Phelem McFadden, and he was painted with a pair of handcuffs on him. Wullum O'Gill had a squint in his right eye, and his thin legs bowed like hoops on a barrel.

If you have ever at night been groping your way through a dark room, and got a sudden, hard bump on the forehead from the edge of the door, you can understand the feelings of the knowledgeable man.

"Take that picture out!" he said, hoarsely, as soon as he could speak. "An' will someone kindly inthrojuice me to the man who med it? Bekase," he says, "I intend to take his life! There was never a crass-eyed O'Gill since the world began," says he.

Think of his horror and surprise when he saw the left eye of Wullum O'Gill twist itself slowly over toward his nose and squint worse than the right eye.

Pretending not to see this, and hoping no one else did, Darby fiercely led the way over to the other wall.

Fronting him stood the handsome picture of Honoria O'Shaughnessy, and she dressed in a suit of tin clothes like the knights of old used to wear—armour I think they calls it.

She held a spear in her hand with a little flag on the blade, and her smile was proud and high.

"Take that likeness out, too," says Darby, very spiteful; "that's not a dacint shuit of clothes for any woman to wear!"

The next minute you might have knocked him down with a feather, for the picture of Honoria O'Shaughnessy opened its mouth and stuck out its tongue at him.

"The supper's getting cowld, the supper's getting cowld!" someone cried at the other end of the picture-gallery. Two big doors were swung open, and glad enough was our poor hero to follow the musicians down to the room where the eating and drinking were to be transacted.

This was a little room with lots of looking-glasses, and it was bright with a thousand candles, and white with the shiniest marble. On the table was boiled beef and radishes and carrots and roast mutton and all kinds of important eating and drinking. Beside there stood fruits and sweets and—but, sure, what is the use in talking?

A high-backed chair stood ready for each of the family, and 'twas a lovely sight to see them all when they were sitting there—Darby at the head, Bridget at the foot, the children—the poor little patriarchs—sitting bolt upright on each side, with a bewigged and befrilled serving-man standing haughty behind every chair.

The eating and drinking would have begun at once—in troth there was already a bit of boiled beef on Darby's plate—only that he spied a little silver bell beside him. Sure, 'twas one like those the quality keep to ring when they want more hot water for their punch, but it puzzled the knowledgeable man, and 'twas the beginnings of his misfortune.

"I wondher," he thought, "if 'tis here for the same raison as the bell is at the Curragh races—do they ring this one so that all at the table will start ating and dhrinking fair, an' no one will have the advantage, or is it," he says to himself again, "to ring whin the head of the house thinks everyone has had enough. Haven't the quality quare ways! I'll be a long time learning them," he says.

He sat silent and puzzling and staring at the boiled beef on his plate, afraid to start in without ringing the bell, and dreading to risk ringing it. The grand servants towered coldly on every side, their chins tilted, but they kept throwing over their shoulders glances so scornful and haughty that Darby shivered at the thought of showing any uncultivation.

While our hero sat thus in uneasy contemplation and smoldering mortification and flurried hesitation, a powdered head was poked over his shoulder, and a soft, beguiling voice said, "Is there anything else you'd wish for?"

The foolish lad twisted in his chair, opened his mouth to speak, and gave a look at the bell; shame rushed to his cheeks, he picked up a bit of the boiled beef on his fork, and to conceal his perturbation gave the misfortunate answer: "I'd wish for a pinch of salt, if you plaze," says he.

'Twas no sooner said than came the crash. Oh, thunderation and murderation, what a roaring crash it was! The lights winked out together at a breath and left a pitchy, throbbing darkness. Overhead and to the sides was a roaring, smashing, crunching noise, like the ocean's madness when the wintry storm breaks against the Kerry shore, and in that roar was mingled the tearing and the splitting of the walls and the falling of the chimneys. But through all this confusion could be heard the shrill, laughing voice of the Leprechaun. "The clever man med his fourth grand wish!" it howled.

Darby—a thousand wild voices screaming and mocking above him—was on his back kicking and squirming and striving to get up, but some load held him down, and something bound his eyes shut.

"Are you kilt, Bridget asthore?" he cried; "where are the childher?" he says.

Instead of answer there suddenly flashed a fierce and angry silence, and its quickness frightened the lad more than all the wild confusion before.

'Twas a full minute before he dared to open his eyes to face the horrors which he felt were standing about him; but when courage enough to look came, all he saw was the night-covered mountain, a purple sky, and a thin, new moon, with one trembling gold star a hand's space above its bosom.

Darby struggled to his feet. Not a stone of the castle was left, not a sod of turf but what was in its old place; every sign of the little cobbler's work had melted like April snow. The very trees Darby had seen pulled up by the roots that same afternoon now stood a waving blur below the new moon, and a nightingale was singing in their branches. A cricket chirped lonesomely on the same fallen log which had hidden the Leprechaun.

"Bridget! Bridget!" Darby called again and again. Only a sleepy owl on a distant hill answered.

A shivering thought jumped into the boy's bewildered soul—maybe the Leprechaun had stolen Bridget and the children.

The poor man turned, and for the last time darted down into the night-filled valley.

Not a pool in the road he waited to go around, not a ditch in his path he didn't leap over, but ran as he never ran before till he reached his own front door.

His heart stood still as he peeped through the window. There were the children crowded around Bridget, who sat with the youngest asleep in her lap before the fire, rocking back and forth, and she crooning a happy, contented baby-song.

Tears of gladness crept into Darby's eyes as he looked in upon her. "God bless her!" he says to himself. "She's the flower of the O'Hagans and the O'Shaughnessys, and she's a proud feather in the caps of the O'Gills and the O'Gradys."

'Twas well he had this happy thought to cheer him as he lifted the door-latch, for the meanest of all the little cobbler's spiteful tricks waited in the house to meet Darby—neither Bridget nor the children remembered a single thing of all that had happened to them during the day. They were willing to make their affidavits that they had been no farther than their own petatie-patch since morning.

THREE

The Convarsion of Father Cassidy

Itold you how on cold winter nights when Bridget and the
children were in bed, old Brian Connors, King of the Fairies,
used to sit visiting at Darby O'Gill's own fireside. But I never
told you of the wild night when the King faced Father Cassidy
there.

*   *   *   *   *   *   *

Darby O'Gill sat at his own kitchen fire the night after
Mrs. Morrisey's burying, studying over a great debate that was
held at her wake.

Half-witted Red Durgan begun it by asking loud and sudden
of the whole company, "Who was the greatest man that ever
lived in the whole worruld? I want to know purtic'lar, an' I'd
like to know at once," he says.

At that the deliberations started.

Big Joey Hooligan, the smith, held out for Julius Sayser,
because Sayser had trounced the widow woman, Clayopathra.

Maurteen Cavanaugh, the little schoolmaster, stood up for
Bonyparte, and wanted to fight Dinnis Moriarity for disputing
against the Frenchman.

Howsomever, the starter of the real excitement was old
Mrs. Clancy. She was not what you'd call a great historian, but
the parish thought her a fine, sensible woman. She said that the

greatest man was Nebbycodnazer, the King of the Jews, who ate grass like a cow and grew fat on it. "Could Julius Sayser or Napoleon Bonyparte do as much?" she asked.

Well, pretty soon everyone was talking at once, hurling at each other, as they would paving-stones, the names of poets and warriors and scholars.

But after all was said and done, the mourners went away in the morning with nothing settled.

So the night after, while Darby was warming his shins before his own turf fire in deep meditation and wise cogitation and calm contemplation over these high conversations, the Master of the Good People flew raging into the kitchen.

"Darby O'Gill, what do you think of your wife Bridget?" says he, fiercely.

"Faix, I don't know what particular thing she's done," says Darby, rubbing his shins and looking troubled, "but I can guess it's something mighty disagrayable. She wore her blue petticoat and her brown shawl when she went away this morning, and I always expect ructions when she puts on that shuit of clothes. Thin agin, she looked so sour and so satisfied whin she came back that I'm worried bad in my mind; you don't know how uncomfortable she can make things sometimes, quiet as she looks," says he.

"And well you may be worried, dacint man!" says the ruler of Sleive-na-mon; "you'll rage and you'll roar whin ye hear me. She wint this day to Father Cassidy and slandhered me outrageous," he says. "She tould him that you and Maureen were colloguing with a little ould, wicked, thieving fairy-man, and that if something wasn't done at once agin him the sowls of both of ye would be desthroyed entirely."

When Darby found 'twas not himself that was being bothered, but only the King, he grew easier in his feelings. "Sure you wouldn't mind women's talk," says he, waving his hand in a lofty way. "Many a good man has been given a bad name by them before this, and will be agin—you're not the first by any manes," says he. "If Bridget makes you a bad repitation, think how many years you have to live it down in. Be sinsible, King!" he says.

"But I do mind, and I must mind!" bawled the little fairy-man, every hair and whisker bristling, "for this minute Father Cassidy is putting the bridle and saddle on his black hunter, Terror; he has a prayer-book in his pocket, and he's coming to read prayers over me and to banish me into the say. Hark! listen to that," he says.

As he spoke, a shrill little voice broke into singing outside the window.

"Oh, what'll you do if the kittle biles over,
Sure, what'll you do but fill it agin;
Ah, what'll you do if your marry a sojer,
But pack up your clothes and go marchin' with him."

"That's the signal!" says the King, all excited; "he's coming and I'll face him here at this hearth, but sorrow foot he'll put over that threshol' till I give him lave. Then we'll have it out face to face like men ferninst this fire!"

When Darby heard those words great fright struck him.

"If a hair of his Riverence's head be harmed," he says, "'tis not you but me and my generation'll be blamed for it. Plaze go back to Sleive-na-mon this night, for pace and quietness sake!" he begged.

While Darby spoke, the fairy-man was fixing one stool on top of another under the window.

"I'll sit at this window," says the Master of the Good People, wagging his head threateningly, "and from there I'll give me ordhers. The throuble he's thrying to bring on others is the throuble I'll throuble him with. If he comes dacint, he'll go dacint; if he comes bothering, he'll go bothered," says he.

Faith, then, your Honour, the King spoke no less than the truth, for at that very minute Terror, as fine a horse as ever followed hounds, was galloping down the starlit road to Darby's house, and over Terror's mane bent as fine a horseman as ever took a six-bar gate—Father Cassidy.

On and on through the moonlight they clattered, till they came in sight of Darby's gate, where, unseen and invisible, a score of the Good People, with thorns in their fists, lay sniggering and laughing, waiting for the horse. Of course the fairies couldn't harm the good man himself, but Terror was completely at their mercy.

"We'll not stop to open the gate, Terror," says his Reverence, patting the beast's neck. "I'll give you a bit of a lift with the bridle-rein, and a touch like that on the flank, and do you clear it, my swallow-bird."

Well, sir, the priest rose in his stirrups, lifted the rein, and Terror crouched for the spring, when, with a sudden snort of pain, the beast whirled round and started like the wind back up the road.

His Reverence pulled the horse to its haunches and swung him round once more facing the cottage. Up on his hind feet went Terror and stood crazy for a second, pawing the air, then with a cry of rage and pain in his throat, the beast turned, made a rush for the hedge at the roadside, and cleared it like an arrow.

Now, just beyond the hedge was a bog so thin that the geese wouldn't walk on it, and so thick that the ducks couldn't swim in it. Into the middle of that cold pond Terror fell with a splash and a crash.

That minute the King climbed down from the window splitting with laughter. "Darby," he says, slapping his knees, "Father Cassidy is floundhering about in the bog outside. He's not hurt, but he's mighty cowld and uncomfortable. Do you go and make him promise not to read any prayers this night, then bring him in. Tell him that if he don't promise, by the piper that played before Moses, he may stay reading his prayers in the bog till morning, for he can't get out unless some of my people go in and help him!" says the King.

Darby's heart began hammering against his ribs as though it were making heavy horseshoes. "If that's so, I'm a ruined man!" he says. "I'd give tunty pounds rather than face him now!" says he.

The distracted lad put his hat on to go out, and then he took it off to stay in. He let a groan out of him that shook all his bones.

"You may save him or lave him," says the King, turning to the window. "I'm going to lave the priest see in a minute what's bothering him. If he's not out of the bog be that time, I'd adwise you to lave the counthry. Maybe you'll only have a pair of cow's horns put on ye, but I think ye'll be kilt," he says. "My own mind's aisy. I wash my hands of him!

"That's the great comfort and adwantage of having your sowl's salwation fixed and sartin one way or the other," says the King, peering out. "Whin you do a thing, bad as it is or good as it may be, your mind is still aisy, bekase—" he turned from the window to look at Darby, but the lad was gone out into the moonlight, and was shrinking and cringing up toward the bog, as though he were going to meet and talk with the ghost of a man he'd murdered. 'Twas a harsher and angrier voice than that of any ghost that came out of a great flopping and splashing in the bog.

Father Cassidy sat with his feet drawn up on Terror, and the horse was half sunk in the mire. At times he urged Terror over to the bank, and just as the beast was raising to step out, with a snort, it'd whirl back again.

He'd try another side, but spur as he might, and whip as he would, the horse'd turn shivering back to the middle of the bog.

"Is that you, Darby O'Gill, you vagebone?" cried his Reverence. "Help me out of this to the dhry land so as I can take the life of you!" he cried.

"What right has anyone to go trespassin' in my bog, mussing it all up an' spiling it?" says Darby, pretending not to recognize the priest; "I keep it private for my ducks and geese, and I'll have the law on you, so I will—Oh, be the powers of Pether, 'tis me own dear Father Cassidy!" he cried.

Father Cassidy, as an answer, reached for a handful of mud, which he aimed and flung so fair and true that three days after Darby was still pulling bits of it from his hair.

"I have a whip I'll keep private for your own two foine legs!" cried his Reverence; "I'll teach you to tell lies to the counthry-side about your being with the fairies, and for deludherin' your own poor wife. I came down this night to eggspose you. But now that's the laste I'll do to you!"

"Faith," says Darby, "if I was with the fairies, 'tis no less than you are this minute, an' if you eggspose me, I'll eggspose you!" With that Darby up and told what was the cause of the botheration.

His Reverence, after the telling, waited not a minute, but kicked the spurs into Terror, and the brave horse headed once more for shore. 'Twas no use. The poor beast turned at last with a cry and floundered back again into the mire.

"You'll not be able to get out, Father acushla," says Darby, "till you promise fair an' firm not to read any prayers over the Good People this night, and never to hurt or molest meself on any account. About this last promise the King is very particular entirely."

"You dundherheaded Booligadhaun!" says Father Cassidy, turning all the blame on Darby; "you mayandherin' Mayrauder of the Sivin Says!" he says. "You big-headed scorpion of the worruld, with bow-legs!" cried he,—and things like that.

"Oh, my! Oh, my! Oh, my!" says Darby, pretending to be shocked, "to think that me own pastor should use sich terrible langwidge! That me own dear Father Cassidy could spake blaggard words like thim! Every dhrop of blood in me is biling with scandalation. Let me beg of you and implore your Riverence never agin to make use of talk like that. It breaks my heart to hear you!" says the villain.

For a few minutes after that Darby was doing nothing but dodging handfuls of mud.

While this was going on, a soft red glow, like that which hangs above the lonely wreaths and forts at night when the fairies are dancing in them, came over the fields. So when Father Cassidy rose in his stirrups, the soft glow was resting on the bog, and there he saw two score of little men in green jackets and brown caps waiting about the pond's edge, and everyone holding a switch in his hands.

The little lads knew well 'twas too dark for the clergyman to read from his book any banishing prayers, and barring having too much fun, the devil a thing they had to fear!

'Twas fresh anger that came to Father Cassidy after the first rush of surprise and wonder. He tried now to get at the Good People, to lay his hands on them. A dozen charges at the bank his Reverence made, and as many times a score of the Little People flew up to meet him and struck the poor beast over the soft nose with their wands till the horse was welted back.

Long after the struggle was proved hopeless it went on till at last the poor beast, trembling and disheartened, refused to mind the spur.

At that Father Cassidy gave up. "I surrender," he said, "an' I promise for the sake of my horse," said he.

The beast himself understood the words, for with that he waded calm and quiet to the dry land and stood shaking himself there among the pack of fairies.

Mighty few words were passed betwixt Darby and Terror's rider as the whole party went up to Darby's stable, the little people following behind quiet and orderly.

It was not long till Terror was nibbling comfortably in a stall, Father Cassidy was drying himself before the kitchen fire, the King and Darby were sitting by the side of the hearth, and two score of the green-cloaked Little People were scattered about the kitchen waiting for the great debate which was sure to come betwixt his Reverence and the head man of the Good People, now that the two had met.

So full was the room that some of the Good People sat on the shelves of the dresser, others lay on the table, their chins in their fists, whilst little Phelim Beg was perching himself on a picture above the hearth. He'd no sooner touched the picture-frame than he let a howl out of him and jumped to the floor. "I'm burned to the bone!" says he.

"No wondher," says the King, looking up; "'twas a picture of St. Patrick you were sitting on."

Phadrig Oge, swinging his heels, balanced himself on the edge of a churn filled with buttermilk, but everyone of them kept wondering eyes fastened on the priest.

And to tell the truth, Father Cassidy at first was more scornful and unpolite than he need be.

"I suppose," says his Reverence, "you do be worrying a good deal about the place you're going to afther the Day of Judgement?" he says, kind of mocking.

"Arrah, now," says the King, taking the pipe from his mouth and staring hard at the clergyman, "there's more than me ought to be studying that question. There's a parish priest I know, and he's not far from here, who ate mate on a fast day, three years ago come Michaelmas, who should be a good lot intherested in that same place," says the King.

The laughing and tittering that followed this hit lasted a minute.

Father Cassidy turned scarlet. "When I ate it I forgot the day!" he cried.

"That's what you tould," says the King, smiling sweet, "but that saying don't help your chanst much. Maybe you failed to say your prayers a year ago last Ayster Monday night for the same rayson?" asked the King, very cool.

At this the laughing broke out again, uproarious, some of the little men holding their sides and tears rolling down their cheeks; two lads began dancing together before the china dishes upon the dresser. But at the height of the merriment there was a cry and a splash, for Phadrig Oge had fallen into the churn.

Before anyone could help him Phadrig had climbed bravely up the churn-dash, hand over hand like a sailor man, and clambered out all white and dripping. "Don't mind me," he says; "go on wid the discoorse!" he cried, shaking himself. The Ruler of the Good People looked vexed.

"I marvel at yez, an' I am ashamed of yez!" he says. "If I'm not able alone for this dayludhered man, yer shoutin' and your gallivantin'll do me no good. Besides, fair play's a jewel, even two agin one ain't fair," says the King. "If I hear another word from one of yez, back to Sleive-na-mon he'll go, an' lay there on the broad of his back, with his heels in the air, for a year and tin days!

"You were about to obsarve, Father Cassidy," says his Majesty, bowing low—"your most obaydient, sir!"

"I was about to say," cried his Reverence, "that you're a friend of Sattin!"

"I'll not deny that," says the King; "what have you to say agin him?"

"He's a rogue and a rapscallion and the inemy of mankind!" thundered Father Cassidy.

"Prove he's a rogue!" cries the King, slapping one hand on the other; "and why shouldn't he be the inemy of mankind? What has mankind iver done for him except to lay the blame of every mane, cowardly thrick of its own on his chowlders. Wasn't it on their account he was put inside of the swine and dhrove into the say? Wasn't it bekase of them he spint sivin days and sivin nights in the belly of a whale, wasn't it—"

"Stop there, now!" says Father Cassidy, pointing his finger; "hould where you are—that was Jonah."

"You're working meracles to make me forget!" shouted the King.

"I'm not!" cried the priest, "and what's more, if you'll agree not to use charms of the black art to help yourself, I'll promise not to work meracles agin you."

"Done! I'll agree," says the King, "and with that bargain I'll go on first, and I'll prove that mankind is the inemy of Sattin."

"Who begun the inmity?" interrupted His Reverence; "who started in be tempting our first parents?"

"Not wishing to make little of a man's relaytions in his own house or to his own face, but your first parents were a poor lot," said the King. "Didn't your first parent turn quane's evidence agin his own wife? Answer me that!"

"Undher the sarcumstances, would ye have him tell a lie whin he was asked?" says the priest right back.

Well, the argument got hotter and hotter until Darby's mind was in splinters. Sometimes he sided with Old Nick, sometimes he was against him. Half of what they said he didn't understand. They talked Theology, Conchology, and Distrology, they hammered each with Jayography, Orthography, and Misnography, they welted each other with Hylosophy, Philosophy, and Thrimosophy. They bounced up and down in their seats, they shouted and got purple in the face. But every argument brought out another nearly as good and twice as loud.

Through all this time the followers of the King sat upon their perches or lay upon the table motionless, like little wooden images with painted green cloaks and brown caps.

Darby, looking from one to the other of them for help to understand the tremendous argument that was going on, felt his brain growing numb. At last it balked like Shamus Free's donkey, and urge as he would, the devil a foot his mind'd stir after the two heroes. It turned at last and galloped back to Mrs. Morrisey's wake.

Now, then, the thought that came into Darby's head as he sat ferninst Father Cassidy and the King was this: "The two wisest persons in Ireland are this minute shouting and disputing before me own turf fire. If I ax them those questions, I'll be wiser than Maurteen Cavanaugh, the schoolmaster, an' twict as wise as any other man in this parish. I'll do it," he says to himself.

He raised the tongs and struck them so loud and quick against the hearth that the two debaters stopped short in their talk to look at him.

"Tell me," he says—"lave off and tell me who was the greatest man that ever lived?" says he.

At that a surprising thing happened. Brian Connors and Father Cassidy, each striving to speak first, answered in the same breath and gave the same name.

"Dan'le O'Connell," says they.

There was at that the instant's silence and stillness which follows a great explosion of gunpowder.

Then every subject of the King started to his feet. "Three cheers for Dan'le O'Connell!" cried little Roderick Dhue. Every brown cap was swung in the air. "Hooray! Hooray! Hooroo!" rang the cheers.

His Reverence and the fairy-chief turned sharp about and stared at each other, delighted and wondering.

Darby struck again with the tongs. "Who was the greatest poet?" says he.

Again the two spoke together. "Tom Moore," says they. The King rubbed his hands and gave a glad side look at the priest. Darby marked the friendly light that was stealing into Father Cassidy's brown eyes. There was great excitement among the Good People up on the cupboard shelves.

On the table little Nial, the wise, was trying to start three cheers for Father Cassidy, when Darby said again: "Who was the greatest warrior?" he says.

The kitchen grew still as death, each of the two heroes waiting for the other.

The King spoke first. "Brian Boru," says he.

"No," says Father Cassidy, half laughing; "Owen Roe O'Nale."

Phadrig Oge jumped from the churn. "Owen Roe forever! I always said it!" cries he. "Look at this man, boys," he says, pointing up to the priest. "There's the making of the foinest bishop in Ireland!"

"The divil a much differ betwixt Owen Roe an' Brian Boru! 'Tis one of them two, an' I don't care which!" says the King.

The priest and the King sank back in their chairs, eyeing each other with admiration.

Darby poured something out of a jug into three brown stone noggins, and then turned hot water from the kettle on top of that again.

Says the King to the clergyman, "You're the cleverest and the knowingest man I've met in five thousand years. That joult you gave me about Jonah was a terror!"

"I never saw your ayquil! If we could only send you to Parliament, you'd free Ireland!" says Father Cassidy. "To think," says he, "that once I used to believe there was no such thing as fairies!"

"That was bekase you were shuperstitious," says the King. "Everyone is so, more or less. I am meself—a little," says he.

Darby was stirring spoons in the three steaming noggins and Father Cassidy was looking troubled. What would his flock say to see him drinking with a little old pagan, who was the friend of Old Nick?

"Your health!" says the King, holding up the cup.

His Reverence took a bowl of the punch, for decency's sake, and stood quiet a minute. At last he says, "Happiness to you and forgiveness to you, and my heart's pity folly you!" says he, raising the noggin to his lips.

He drained the cup thoughtful and solemn, for he didn't know rightly whether 'twas a venial sin or mortal sin he'd committed by the bad example he was giving Darby. "I wisht I could do something for yez," he says, putting on his cloak, "but I have only pity and kind wishes to give you!"

He turned again when his hand was on the doorknob, and was going to say something else, but changed his mind, and went out to where Darby was holding the horse.

Meanwhile, the Little People were consulting eager in a knot beside the fireplace, until the King broke away and followed Father Cassidy out.

"Wait a minute!" the fairy says. "There's somethin' important your Riverence should know about," he says. "There's two speckled hins that sthrayed away from your own door over to the black pond, an' they've been there this twelvemonth. I'm loathe to say it, but in yer own mind your honour accused Bothered Bill Donahue, the tinker, with takin' them. Well, they've raised two great clutches of chickens an' they're all yours. We thought we'd tell ye," he says.

"An' last Chewsday night Nancy Burke bate her husband Dicky for being 'toxicated. I think she bate him too scan'lous," says little Nial, the fiddler, coming out. "An' Dicky is too proud to complain of her to your honour. He says 'twould be makin' a kind of informer out of himself. But maybe she'll bate him agin, so I thought to mintion it," he says.

With that Phadrig Oge broke in from where he stood on the threshold: "Tom Healey's family, up the mountainy way, is all down with the faver; they have no one to send worrud!" cried Phadrig; "Your honour ought to know about it," he says.

By this time the Good People were all outside, crowded about the horse, and each one excited, shouting up some friendly information.

Father Cassidy, from Terror's back, sat smiling down kind, first on this one, then on that, and then on the other.

"Wisha!" says he, "ain't ye the kindly crachures! I've heard more news of me own parish in the last foive minutes than I'd have learned in a twelvemonth. But there's one thing I'd liked mighty well to know. Maybe yez could tell me," says he, "who committed the mystarious crime in this parish a year ago last Christmas? Who stole the six shillin's from ould Mrs. Frawley? She counted them at Mrs. McGee's, and she felt them in her pocket at Mrs. Donovan's; the crowd jostled her at the chapel door, an' afther that they were gone," he says.

Well, the fairies were splitting with laughter as he spoke.

"No one stole thim at all," says Shaun Rhue, the tears of merriment rolling down his face. "The disraymemberin' woman only aymagins she counted thim at Mrs. McGee's an' felt thim at Mrs. Donovan's. She was only thinkin' about the money at thim places, an' that's how she got the ideeh. She hid the shillin's in the blue taypot with the broken spout, that stands in the left-han' corner of the mayhogany dhresser, an' thin forgot it entirely," he says.

"Well, look at that, now," says the priest, "an' all the turmile there's been about that same six shillin's, an' she afther hidin' them in the taypot herself. Now isn't there something I can do in rayturn for all your kindness?" he says.

"There's one thing," says King Brian Connors, looking a good deal confused. "If your Riverence could just as well—if it'd be no positive inconvaynience—we'd like mightily for ye not to be singin' pious hymns as you go riding along the highway afther dark. If you'd sing ballads, now, or Tom Moore's melodies. You mane no harrum, of course, as it is, but last week you broke up a dance we were having at Murray's rath, an' Saturday night you put a scatther on a crowd of us as we were coming by McGrath's meadow," he says, anxious.

'Twas a queer bargain for a clergyman to make, and faith it went against his conscience, but he hadn't the heart to refuse. So he bent down and shook the King's hand. "I promise," he says.

A wild, shrill cheer broke from the throng of Little People.

"Now I'll go home an' lave yez in peace," says Father Cassidy, gripping his bridle-rein. "I came yer inemy, but I'm converted. I'll go back yer friend," he says.

"Ye won't go home alone, we'll escorch ye!" shouted Phadrig Oge.

*   *   *   *   *   *   *

Wullum Fagin, the poacher, was sneaking home that night about one o'clock, with a bag full of rabbits under his arm, when hearing behind him the beat of horse's hoofs and the sound of melodious music, he jumped into the ditch and lay close within the shadow.

Who should come cantering up the starlit road but Father Cassidy, on his big black hunter, Terror.

Wullum looked for the musicianers who were singing and playing the entrancing music, but sorra one could he see, and what was more, the sounds came from the air high above Father Cassidy's head.

"'Tis the angels guarding the good man," says Wullum.

Sure 'twas only the Good People escorting his Reverence from Darby O'Gill's house, and to cheer him on his way, singing the while, "Believe me, if all those endearing young charms."

FOUR

How the Fairies Came to Ireland

The most lonesome bridle-path in all Ireland leads from Tom Healey's cottage down the sides of the hills, along the edge of the valley, till it reaches the high-road that skirts the great mountain, Sleive-na-mon.

One blustering, uneasy night Father Cassidy, on his way home from a sick-call, rode over that same path. It wasn't strange that the priest, as his horse ambled along, should be thinking of that other night in Darby O'Gill's kitchen—the night when he met with the Good People; for there, off to the left, towered and threatened Sleive-na-mon, the home of the fairies.

The dismal old mountain glowered toward his Reverence, its dark look saying, plain as spoken words: "How dare ye come here; how dare ye?"

"I wondher," says Father Cassidy to himself, looking up at the black hill, "if the Good People are fallen angels, as some do be saying.

"Why were they banished from heaven? It must have been a great sin entirely they committed, at any rate, for at the same time they were banished, the power to make a prayer was taken from them. That's why to say a pious word to a fairy is like trowing scalding wather on him. 'Tis a hard pinnance that's put on the poor crachures. I wisht I knew what 'twas for," he says.

He was going on pondering in that way, while Terror was picking his steps, nervous, among the stones of the road, when suddenly a frowning, ugly rock seemed to jump and stand ferninst them at a turn of the path.

Terror shied at it, stumbled wild, and then the most aggravating of all bothersome things happened—the horse cast a shoe and went stone lame.

In a second the priest had leaped to the ground and picked up the horseshoe.

"Wirra! Wirra!" says he, lifting the lame foot, "why did you do it, alannah? 'Tis five miles to a smith an' seven miles to your own warm stable."

The horse, for answer, reached down and touched with his soft nose the priest's cheek; but the good man looked reproachful into the big brown eyes that turned sorrowful to his own.

With the shoe in his hand the priest was standing fretting and helpless on the lonesome hillside, wondering what he'd do at all at all, when a sudden voice spoke up from somewhere near Terror's knees. "The top of the avinin' to your Riverence," it said; "I'm sorry for your bad luck," says the voice.

Looking down, Father Cassidy saw a little cloaked figure, and caught the glint of a gold crown. 'Twas Brian Connors, the King of the Fairies, himself, that was in it.

His words had so friendly a ring in them that the clergyman smiled in answering, "Why, thin, good fortune to you, King Brian Connors!" says the good man, "an' save you kindly. What wind brought you here?" he says.

The King spoke back free and pleasant. "The boys tould me you were comin' down the mountainy way, and I came up just in time to see your misfortune. I've sent for Shaun Rhue, our own farrier—there's no betther in Ireland; he'll be here in a minute, so don't worry," says the King.

The priest came so near saying "God bless ye!" that the King's hair rose on his head. But Father Cassidy stopped in the nick of time, changed his course, and steered as near a blessing as he could without hurting the Master of the Good People. "Well, may you never hear of throuble," he says, "till you're wanted to its wake," says he.

"There's no throuble tonight at any rate," says the King, "for while Shaun is fixing the baste we'll sit in the shelter of that rock yonder; there we'll light our pipes and divart our minds with pleasant discoorsin' and wise convarsaytion."

While the King spoke, two green-cloaked little men were making a fire for the smith out of twigs. So quick did they work, that by the time the priest and the fairy-man could walk over to the stone and sit themselves in the shelter, a thousand gold sparks were dancing in the wind, and the glimmer of a fine blaze fought with the darkness.

Almost as soon, clear and purty, rang the cheerful sound of an anvil, and through the swaying shadows a dozen busy little figures were working about the horse. Some wore leather aprons and held up the horse's hoof whilst Shaun fitted the red-hot shoe; others blew the bellows or piled fresh sticks on the fire; all joking, laughing, singing, or tricking; one couldn't tell whether 'twas playing or working they were.

After lighting their pipes and paying each other an armful of compliments, the Master of Sleive-na-mon and the clergyman began a serious discourse about the delights of fox-hunting, which led to the consideration of the wonderful wisdom of racing horses and the disgraceful deterioration of the Skibberbeg hounds.

Father Cassidy related how when Ned Blaze's steeplechasing horse had been entered for the Connemara Cup, and found out at the last minute that Ned feared to lay a bet on him, the horse felt himself so stabbed to the heart with shame by his master's distrust that he threw his jockey, jumped the wall, and head in the air, galloped home.

The King then told how at a great hunting meet, when three magistrates and two head excises officers were in the chase, that thief of the world, Let-Erin-Remember, the chief hound of the Skibberbeg pack, instead of following the fox, led the whole hunt up over the mountain to Patrick McCaffrey's private still. The entire country-side were dry for a fortnight after.

Their talk in that way drifted from one pleasant subject to another, till Father Cassidy, the sly man, says easy and careless, "I've been tould," says he, "that before the Good People were banished from heaven yez were all angels," he says.

The King blew a long thin cloud from betwixt his lips, felt his whiskers thoughtful for a minute, and then said: "No," he says, "we were not exactly what you might call angels. A rale angel is taller nor your chapel."

"Will you tell me what they're like?" asked Father Cassidy, very curious.

"I'll give you an idee by comparison what they're like," the King says. "They're not like a chapel, and they're not like a three, an' they're not like the ocean," says he. "They're different from a giont—a great dale different—and they're dissembler to an aygle; in fact, you'd not mistake one of them for anything you'd ever seen before in your whole life. Now you have a purty good ideeh what they're like," says he.

"While I think of it," says the fairy-man, a vexed frown wrinkling over his forehead, "there's three young bachelors in your own parish that have a foolish habit of callin' their colleens angels whin they's not the laste likeness—not the laste. If I were you, I'd preach agin it," says he.

"Oh, I dunno about that!" says Father Cassidy, fitting a live coal on his pipe. "The crachures must say thim things. If a young bachelor only talks sensible to a sensible colleen he has a good chanst to stay a bachelor. An' thin agin, a gossoon who'll talk to his sweetheart about the size of the petatie crop'll maybe bate her when they're both married. But this has nothing to do with your historical obserwaytions. Go on, King," he says.

"Well, I hate foolishness, wherever it is," says the fairy. "Howsumever, as I was saying, up there in heaven they called us the Little People," he says; "millions of us flocked together, and I was the King of them all. We were happy with one another as birds of the same nest, till the ruction came on betwixt the black and the white angels.

"How it all started I never rightly knew, nor wouldn't ask for fear of getting implicayted. I bade all the Little People keep to themselves thin, because we had plenty of friends in both parties, and wanted throuble with nayther of them.

"I knew Ould Nick well; a civiller, pleasanter spoken sowl you couldn't wish to meet—a little too sweet in his ways, maybe. He gave a thousand favours and civilities to my subjects, and now that he's down, the devil a word I'll say agin him."

"I'm agin him," says Father Cassidy, looking very stern; "I'm agin him an' all his pumps an' worruks. I'll go bail that in the ind he hurt yez more than he helped yez!"

"Only one thing I blame him for," says the King; "he sajooced from the Little People my comrade and best friend, one Thaddeus Flynn be name. And the way that it was, was this: Thaddeus was a warm-hearted little man, but monsthrous high-spirited as well as quick-tempered. I can shut me eyes now and in me mind see him thripping along, his head bent, his pipe in his mouth, his hands behind his back. He never wore a waistcoat, but kept always his green body-coat buttoned. A tall caubeen was set on the back of his head, with a sprig of green shamrock in the band. There was a thin rim of black whuskers undher his chin."

Father Cassidy, lifting both hands in wonder, said: "If I hadn't baptised him, and buried his good father before him, I'd swear 'twas Michael Pether McGilligan of this parish you were dayscribin'," says he.

"The McGilligans ain't dacint enough, nor rayfined enough, nor proud enough to be fairies," says the King, waving his pipe scornful. "But to raysume and to continue," he says.

"Thaddeus and I used frayquint a place they called the battlements or parypets,—which was a great goold wall about the edge of heaven, and which had wide steps down on the outside face, where one could sit pleasant avenings and hang his feet over, or where one'd stand before going to take a fly in the fresh air for himself.

"Well, agra, the night before the great battle Thady and I were sitting on the lowest step, looking down into league upon league of nothing, and talking about the world, which was suxty thousand miles below, and hell, which was tunty thousand miles below that agin, when who should come blusthering over us, his black wings hiding the sky, and a long streak of lightning for a spear in his fist, but Ould Nick.

"'Brian Connors, how long are you going to be down-throdden and thrajooced and looked down upon—you and your subjects?' says he.

"'Faix, thin, who's doing that to us?' asks Thady, standing up and growing excited.

"'Why,' says Ould Nick, 'were you made little pigmies to be the laugh and the scorn and the mock of the whole world?' he says, very mad; 'why weren't you made into angels, like the rest of us?' he says.

"'Musha,' cries Thady, 'I never thought of that.'

"'Are you a man or a mouse; will you fight for your rights?' says Sattin. 'If so, come with me and be one of us. For we'll bate them black and blue tomorrow!' he says. Thady needed no second axing.

"'I'll go with ye, Sattin, me dacint man,' cried he. 'Wirra! Wirra! To think of how down-throdden we are!' And with one spring Thady was on Ould Nick's chowlders, and the two flew away like a humming-bird riding on the back of an aygle.

"'Take care of yerself, Brian,' says Thady, 'and come over to see the fight; I'm to be in it, and I extind you the inwitation,' he says.

"In the morning the battle opened; one line of black angels stretched clear across heaven, and faced another line of white angels, with a walley between.

"Everyone had a spaking-trumpet in his hand, like you see in the pictures, and they called each other hard names across the walley. As the white angels couldn't swear or use bad langwidge, Ould Nick's army had at first in that way a great advantage. But when it came to hurling hills and shying tunderbolts at aich other, the black angels were bate from the first.

"Poor little Thaddeus Flynn stood amongst his own, in the dust and the crash and the roar, brave as a lion. He couldn't hurl mountains, nor was he much at flinging lightning bolts, but at calling hard names he was aquil to the best.

"I saw him take off his coat, trow it on the ground, and shake his pipe at a thraymendous angel. 'You owdacious villain,' he cried, 'I dare you to come half way over!' he says.

"My, oh, my, whin the armies met together in the rale handy grips, it must have been an illegent sight!" says Father Cassidy. "'Tis a wondher you kep' out of it," says he.

"I always belayved," says the King, "that if he can help it, no one should fight whin he's sure to get hurted, onless it's his juty to fight. To fight for the mere sport of it, when a throuncin' is sartin, is wasting your time and hurtin' your repitation. I know there's plenty thinks different," he says, pointing his pipe. "I may be wrong, an' I won't argyfy the matther. 'Twould have been betther for myself that day if I had acted on the other principle.

"Howsumever, be the time that everybody was sidestepping mountains and dodging tunderbolts, I says to myself, says I, 'This is no place fer you or the likes of you.' So I took all me own people out to the battlements and hid them out of the way on the lower steps. We'd no sooner got placed when—whish! a black angel shot through the air over our heads, and began falling down, down, down, and down, till he was out of sight. Then a score of his friends came tumbling over the battlements; imagetly hundreds of others came whirling, and purty soon it was raining black wings down into the gulf.

"In the midst of the turmile who should come jumping down to me, all out of breath, but Thady. 'It's all over, Brian; we're bate scandalous,' he says, swinging his arms for a spring, and balancing himself up and down on the edge of the steps. 'Maybe you wouldn't think it of me, Brian Connors, but I'm a fallen angel,' says he.

"'Wait a bit, Thaddeus Flynn!' says I. 'Don't jump!' I says.

"'I must jump,' he says, 'or I'll be trun,' says he.

"The next thing I knew he was swirling and darting and shooting a mile below me.

"And I know," says the King, wiping his eyes with his cloak, "that when the Day of Judgement comes I'll have at laste one friend waiting for me below to show me the coolest spots and the pleasant places.

"The next minute up came the white army with presners—angels, black and white, who had taken no side in the battle, but had stood apart like ourselves.

"'A man,' says the Angel Gabriel, 'who, for fear of his skin, won't stand for the right when the right is in danger, may not desarve hell, but he's not fit for heaven. Fill up the stars with these cowards and throw the lavins into the say!' he ordhered.

"With that he swung a lad in the air, and gave him a fling that sent him ten miles out intil the sky. Every other good angel follyed shuit, and I watched thousands go, till they faded like a stretch of black smoke a hundred miles below.

"The Angel Gabriel turned and saw me, and I must confess I shivered. 'Well, King Brian Connors,' says he, 'I hope you see that there's such a thing as being too wise and too cute and too ticklish of yourself. I can't send you to the stars, bekase they're full, and I won't send you to the bottomless pit so long as I can help it. I'll send yez all down to the world. We're going to put human beans on it purty soon, though they're going to turn out to be blaggards, and at last we'll have to burn the place up. Afther that, if you're still there, you and yours must go to purdition, for it's the only place left for you.'

"'You're too hard on the little man,' says the Angel Michael, coming up—St. Michael was ever the out-spoken, friendly person—'sure, what harm, or what hurt, or what good could he have done us? And can you blame the poor little crachures for not interfering?'

"'Maybe I was too harsh,' says the Angel Gabriel, 'but being saints, when we say a thing we must stick to it. Howsumever, I'll let him settle in any part of the world he likes, and I'll send there the kind of human beans he'd wish most for.

Now, give your ordher,' he says to me, taking out his book and pencil, 'and I'll make for you the kind of people you'd like to live among.'

"'Well,' says I, 'I'd like the men honest and brave, and the women good.'

"'Very well,' he says, writing it down; 'I've got that—go on.'

"'And I'd like them full of jollity and sport, fond of racing and singing and hunting and fighting, and all such innocent divarsions.'

"'You'll have no complaint about that,' says he.

"'And,' says I, 'I'd like them poor and parsecuted, bekase when a man gets rich there's no more fun in him.'

"'Yes, I'll fix that. Thrue for you,' says Angel Gabriel, writing.

"'And I don't want them to be Christians,' says I; 'make them Haythens or Pagans, for Christians are too much worried about the Day of Judgement.'

"'Stop there! Say no more!' says the saint. 'If I make as fine a race of people as that I won't send them to hell to plaze you, Brian Connors.'

"'At laste,' says I, 'make them Jews.'

"'If I made them Jews,' he says, slowly screwing up one eye to think, 'how could you keep them poor? No, no!' he said, shutting up the book, 'go your ways; you have enough.'

"I clapped me hands, and all the Little People stood up and bent over the edge, their fingers pointed like swimmers going to dive. 'One, two, three,' I shouted, and with that we took the leap.

"We were two years and tunty-six days falling before we raiched the world. On the morning of the next day we began our sarch for a place to live. We thravelled from north to south and from ayst to west. Some grew tired and dhropped off in Spain, some in France, and others agin in different parts of the world. But the most of us thravelled ever and ever till we came to a lovely island that glimmered and laughed and sparkled in the middle of the say.

"'We'll stop here,' I says; 'we needn't sarch farther, and we needn't go back to Italy or Swizzerland, for of all places on the earth this island is the nearest like heaven; and in it the County Clare and the County Tipperary are the purtiest spots of all.' So we hollowed out the great mountain Sleive-na-mon for our home, and there we are till this day."

The King stopped a while, and sat holding his chin in his hands. "That's the thrue story," he says, sighing pitiful. "We took sides with nobody, we minded our own business, and we got trun out for it," says he.

So interested was Father Cassidy in the talk of the King that the singing and hammering had died out without his knowing, and he hadn't noticed at all how the darkness had thickened in the valley, and how the stillness had spread over the hillside. But now, when the chief of the fairies stopped, the good man, half frightened at the silence, jumped to his feet and turned to look for his horse.

Beyond the dull glow of the dying fire a crowd of Little People stood waiting, patient and quiet, holding Terror, who champed restless at his bit, and beat impatient with his hoof on the hard ground.

As the priest looked toward them, two of the little men wearing leather aprons moved out from the others, leading the beast slow and careful over to where the good man stood beside the rock.

"You've done me a faver this night," says the clergyman, gripping with his bridle-hand the horse's mane, "an' all I have to pay it back with'd only harry you an' make you oncomfortable, so I'll not say the words," he says.

"No faver at all," says the King, "but before an hour there'll be lyin' on your own threshold a faver in the shape of a bit of as fine bacon as ever laughed happy in the middle of biling turnips. We borryed it last night from a magisthrate named Blake, who lives up in the County Wexford," he says.

The clergyman had swung himself into the saddle. "I'd be loathe to say anything disrayspectful," he says quick, "or to hurt sensitive feelings, but on account of my soul's sake I couldn't ate anything that was come by dishonest," he says.

"Bother and botheration, look at that, now!" says the King. "Every thrade has its drawbacks, but I never rayalized before the hardship of being a parish priest. Can't we manage it some way? Couldn't I put it some place where you might find it, or give it to a friend who'd sent it to you?"

"Stop a minute," says Father Cassidy. "Up at Tom Healey's I think there's more hunger than sickness, more nade for petaties than for physic. Now, if you send that same bit of bacon—"

"Oh, ho!" says the King, with a dry cough, "the Healeys have no sowls to save, the same as parish priests have."

"I'm a poor, wake, miserable sinner," says the priest, hanging his head; "I fall at the first temptation. Don't send it," says he.

"Since you forbid me, I'll send it," says the King, chuckling. "I'll not be ruled by you. Tomorrow the Healeys'll have five tinder-hearted heads of cabbage, makin' love in a pot to the finest bit of bacon in Tipperary—that is, unless you do your juty an' ride back to warn them. Raymember their poor sowls," says he, "an' don't forget your own," he says.

The priest sat uneasy in the saddle. "I'll put all the raysponsibility on Terror," he says. "The baste has no sowl to lose. I'll just drop the reins on his neck; if he turns and goes back to Healey's I'll warn them; if he goes home let it be on his own conscience."

He dropped the reins, and the dishonest beast started for home immediately.

But after a few steps Father Cassidy drew up and turned in the saddle. Not a soul was in sight; there was only the lonely road and the lonesome hillside; the last glimmer of the fairy-fire was gone, and a curtain of soft blackness had fallen betwixt him and where the blaze had been.

"I bid you good night, Brian Connors!" the priest cried.

From somewhere out of the darkness a voice called back to him, "Good night, Your Riverence!"

FIVE

The Adventures of King Brian Connors

Part I. The King and the Omadhaun*

Did your honour ever hear how Anthony Sullivan's goat came to join the fairies?

Well, it's a queer story and a wandering, quarrelsome story, as a tale about a goat is sure to be. Howsomever, in the home of the Good People—which, as you know, is the hollow heart of the great mountain Sleive-na-mon—Anthony Sullivan's goat lives and prospers to this day, a pet and a hero among the fairies.

And this is the way it came about:

All the world knows how for months Darby O'Gill and his pretty sister-in-law, Maureen McGibney, were kept prisoners by the Good People; and how, after they were released by the King, that same little fairy, King Brian Connors, used often to visit them and sit with them colloguing and debating and considering in Darby O'Gill's kitchen.

One lonesome December night, when Bridget and the children were away visiting Bridget's father at Ballingher, and the angry blast was screaming and drifting the first white flakes of winter around Darby's house, then it was that Darby O'Gill, Brian Connors, the King of the Good People, and Maureen McGibney sat with their heads together before the blazing hearth.

*Omadhaun, a foolish fellow

The King, being not much higher than your two hands, sat on the child's stool betwixt the other two, his green cloak flung back from his shoulders, and the gold crown on his head glistening in the firelight.

It was a pleasant sight to watch them there in the flickering hearth glow. From time to time, as he talked, the old King patted Maureen's hands and looked smiling up into her pretty gray eyes. They had been discoursing on the subject of Troubles and Tribulations.

"Arrah! You ought to be the happy man, King," Darby says, sipping his noggin of punch, "with no silly woman to ordher you or to cross you or to belittle you. Look at meself. Afther all the rayspect I've climbed into from being with the fairies, and afther all the knowledge I've got from them, there's one person in this parish who has no more riverence for me now than she had the first day she met me—sometimes not so much, I'm thinking," he says, hurt-like.

"I've seen the workings of families during more than five thousand years," says the little King, "so you needn't tell me who that one person is, me poor man—'tis your own wife, Bridget."

"Thrue for you! Whin it's the proud woman she ought to be this day to have the likes of me for a husband," says Darby. "Ah, then, you ought to be the happy man, whatever wind blows," he sighed again; "when you see a fat pig you like, you take it without so much as saying by your lave; if you come upon a fine cow or a good horse, in a twinkling you have it in Sleive-na-mon. A girl has a good song with her, a boy has a nimble foot for a jig, or an ould woman a smooth tongue for a tale, and, whisk! they're gone into the heart of the mountain to sing or dance for you, or to beguile you with ould tales until the Day of Judgement."

The King shook his head slowly, and drew a long face. "Maybe we ought to be happy," says he. "'Tis thrue there's no sickness in Sleive-na-mon, nor worry for tomorrow, nor fret for one's childher, nor parting from friends, or things like that, but throuble is like the dhrifting snow outside, Darby; it falls on the cottage and it covers the castle with the same touch, and once in a while it sifts into Sleive-na-mon."

"In the name of goodness!" cries Darby, surprised, "is there anything in the whole world you can't have for the wishing it?"

The King took off his gold crown and began polishing it with his sleeve to hide his nervousness. "I'll tell you a saycret," he whispered, bending over toward Darby, and speaking slow. "In Sleive-na-mon our hearts are just breaking for something we can't get; but that's one thing we'd give the worruld for."

"Oh, King, what in the livin' worruld can it be?" cried Maureen.

"I'd give the teeth out of me head if I could only own a goat," says the King, looking as though he were going to cry.

"Man alive!" says Darby, dropping the poker, "the counthry-side is full of goats, and all you have to do is to take your pick and help yourself. You're making game of us, King."

The King shook his head. "The Good People have been thrying for years to capture one," says he. "I've been bunted into ditches by the villains; I've been trun over hedges by them; I had to leap on the back of Anthony Sullivan's goat, and with two hundred of me subjects in full cry behind, ride him all night long, houlding by his horns to kape him from getting at me and disthroying me entirely. The jumps he took with me that night were thraymendous. It was from the cow-shed to the sthraw-stack, from the sthraw-stack to the house-top, and from there down to the ground agin, and then hooraying an' hoorooing, a race up the mountain-side. But," says the King, kind of sniffling and turning to the fire, "we love the ground he walks upon," says he.

"Tare an' ouns!" says Darby, "why don't you put your spell on one of them?"

"You don't know them," says the King. "We can't put the black spell on thim—they're not Christian bastes, like pigs or cows. Whin it comes to animals, we can only put our come 'ither on cattle and horses, and such as are Christian animals, ye know. In his mind and in his heart a goat is a pagen. He wouldn't ask any betther divarsion than for me to thry and lay me hands on him," says the King, wiping his eyes.

"But," says he again, standing up on the stool and holding his pipe over his head, "Anthony Sullivan's goat is the gallusest baste that roams the fields! There's more fun in him, and no more fear in him, than in a yallow lion. He'd do anything for sport; he'd bunt the King of Russia, he'd ba-a at a parish priest, out of pure, rollicking diviliment," says the King. "If the Good People had a friend, a rale friend," says he, looking hard at Darby, "that wouldn't be afeard to go into our home within the mountain once more, just once, and bring with him that goat—"

"Say no more," says Darby, hoarsely, and turning white with fear—"say no more, Brian Connors! Not all the goold in Sleive-na-mon would tempt me there agin! It's make a presner of me for ever you would. I know your thricks."

The look of scorn the little man flung at Darby would have withered the trees.

"I might have known it," he says, sitting down disgusted. "I was a fool for hoping you would," says he. "There's no more spirit in ye nor sinse of gratichude than in a hin. Wait till!—" and he shook his fist.

"Don't blame the lad," cried Maureen patting the King's head, sootheringly; "sure, why should the like of a wondherful man, such as you, who has lived five thousand years, and knows everything, compare your wit or your spirit or your sinse with the likes of us poor crachures that only stay here a few hours and thin are gone for ever?" This she cried, craftily, flattering the old man. "Be aisy on him, King, acushla!" says she, coaxing.

Well, the little man, being soothered, sat down again. "Maybe I was too hard," he says, "but to tell the truth, the life is just bothered out of me, and my temper is runed these days with an omadhaun we've taken lately; I don't know what to do with him. Talk of throuble! He mopes and mourns and moothers in spite of all we can do. I've even tould him where the crocks of goold are hid—"

"You haven't tould me that," cries Darby, quickly.

"No," says the King, looking at him sideways.

"At laste not yit," says Darby, looking sideways at the King.

"Not yit, nor will I fer a long time yitter, you covetous, ungrateful spalpeen!" snapped the fairy.

"Well," said he, paying no more attention to Darby, "this young omadhaun is six feet high in his stockings, and as foine a looking lad as you'll see in a day's walk. Now what do you think he's mourning and crooning for?"

"Faix, I dunno," answered Darby. "Maybe it's a horse or a dog or a cow, or maybe a pair of pigs."

"You've not hit it," said the Ruler of the Good People; "it's a colleen. And him having a college education, too."

"Troth, thin," said Darby, with a knowledgeable wag of his head, "some of them larned students are as foolish in that way as ignorant people. I once met a tinker named Larry McManus, who knew the jography from cover to cover, and still he had been married three times."

"Poor gossoon! Who is the omadhaun?" asked Maureen, not minding Darby.

"He's no less," said the King, "than Roger O'Brien, a son of ould Bob O'Brien, who was the richest and proudest man in the County Tipperary. Ould Bob thraces his ancestors for five hundhred years, and he owns a mile of land and has forty tenants. He had no child but this omadhaun."

"And who is the colleen? Some grand Princess, I suppose," said Maureen.

"There was the whole throuble," answered the little man. "Why, she's no one at all, but a little white-cheeked, brown-eyed, black-haired girl named Norah Costello, belonging to one of his own tenants on the domain. It all came from eddicatin' people above their station."

"Faix," Darby says, "there's Phelem Brady, the stonecutter, a fine, dacint man he was till he made up his mind to larn the history of Ireland from ind to ind. When he got so far as where the Danes killed Brian Boru he took to dhrink, and the divil a ha'porth's good he's been ever since. But lade on with your discoorse, King," says he, waving his noggin of punch.

At this the King filled his pipe, Maureen threw fresh turf on the fire, and the wind drew the sparks dancing up the chimney. Now and then while the King talked, some of the fairies outside rapped on the window-panes and pressed their little faces against the glass to smile and nod at those within, then scurried busily off again into the darkness. Once the wail of a child rose above the cry of the storm and Maureen caught the flash of a white robe against the window-pane.

"It's a child we've taken this night from one Judy Casey down in Mayo," says King Brian Connors. "But fill my noggin with fresh punch, Maureen, and dhraw closer till I tell you about the omadhaun." And the Master of the Good People crossed his legs and settled into telling the story, comfortable as comfortable could be.

"The way the throuble began was foine and innocent as the day is long," said the King. "Five or six years ago—it was on the day Roger was first sent to college at Dublin—Misther and Misthress O'Brien, mighty lonesome an' down-hearted, were dhriving over the estate whin who should they spy standing, modest and timid, at her own gate, but purty little Norah Costello. Though the child was only fourteen years old, Misthress O'Brien was so taken with her wise, gentle ways that Norah next day was sint for to come up to the big house to spind an hour amusing the Misthress. There was the rock they all split on.

"Every day afther for a month the little girl went visiting there. At the end of that time Misthress O'Brien grew so fond of her that Norah was brought to the big house to live. Ould Bob liked the little girl monsthrous well, so they put fine clothes on her until in a couple of years one couldn't tell her from a rale lady, whether he met her in the house or at the crossroad.

"Only every Saturday night she'd put on a little brown poplin dhress and go to her father's cottage, and stay there helping her mother till Monday or maybe Chewsday. 'For I mustn't get proud-hearted,' she'd say, 'or lose the love I was born to, for who can tell whin I'll need it,' says she."

"A wise girl," says Darby.

"A dear colleen," says Maureen.

"Well, every summer me brave Roger came home from college, and the two rode together afther the hounds, or sailed his boat or roved the woods, and the longest summer days were too short entirely to suit the both of them.

"Although she had a dozen young fellows courting her—some of them gentlemen's sons—the divil an eye she had for anyone except Roger; and although he might pick from twinty of the bluest-blooded ladies in Ireland any day he liked, Norah was his one delight.

"Every servant on the place knew how things were going, but the ould man was so blind with pride that he saw nothing at all; stranger than all, the two childher believed that ould Bob guessed the way things were with them an' was plazed with them. A worse mistake was never made. He never dhramed that his son Roger would think of any girl without a fortune or a title.

"Misthress O'Brien must have known, but, being tendher-hearted and loving and, like all women, a trifle weak-minded, hoped, in spite of rayson, that her husband would consint to let the childher marry. Knowing ould Bob as she knew him, that was a wild thought for Misthress O'Brien to have; for if ever there was a stiffer, bittherer, prouder, more unforgiving, boistherous man I haven't seen him, and I've lived five thousand years."

Darby, scowling mighty important, raised his hand. "Whist a bit," he says; "you raymind me of the ballad about Lord Skipperbeg's lovely daughter and the farmer's only son." Stretching his legs and wagging his head, he sang:

"Her cheeks were like the lily white,
    Her neck was like the rose."

"Oh, my! oh, my!" said the King, surprised, "was her neck as red as that?"

"By no manes," said Darby. "I med a mistake; 'twas this away:

"Her neck was like the lily white,
    Her cheeks were like the rose,
She quickly doffed her silk attire
    And donned a yeoman's clothes.

"'Rise up, rise up, my farmer's son,
    Rise up thrue love,' says she,
'We'll fly acrost the ragin' main
    Unto Amer-i—'"

"Have done your fooling, Darby," says Maureen; "you have the King bothered."

"I wisht you hadn't shtopped him, agra," says the King. "I niver heard that song before, an' it promised well. I'm fond of love songs," he says.

"But the omadhaun," coaxed the colleen.

"I forgot where I was," the King says, scratching his head. "But, spaking of ould Bob," he went on, "no one ever thought how evil and bitther he could be, until his son, the foolish lad, a few days before the ind of his schooling, wrote to the father that he wanted to marry Norah whin he came home, and that he would be home in a few days, he thought. He was breaking the news aisy to the family, d'ye see!

"'Whew! Hullabaloo! Out of the house with her—the sly, conniving hussy!' shouted ould Bob, whin he read the letter. 'Into the road with all we've given her! Pull the roof off

Costello's house and dhrive off the place his whole brood of outraygeous villians!'

"So they packed Norah's boxes—faix, an' many a fine dhress was in them, too—and bade her begone. The Misthress slipped a bag of goold sovereigns with a letther into one of the chests. Norah took the letther, but she forbade them sending so much as a handkerchief afther her.

"She wouldn't even ride in the coach that the Misthress had waiting for her outside the grand gate; and all alone, in her brown poplin dhress, she marched down the gravel path, proud, like a queen going to be crowned. Nor did she turn her head when the servants called blessings afther her; but oh, asthore, her face was marble white; and whin she was on her way down the lonely high-road how she cried!

"'Twas a bitther time entirely, the night young Roger came home, and hearing of all this, rushed up the stairs to face his father. What happened betwixt them there no one knows, only they never passed aich other a friendly look nor gave one to the other a pleasant word from that good hour to this.

"To make matthers worse, that same night young Roger wint and axed Norah Costello to marry him. But all the counthry-side knows how the girl rayfused him, saying she wouldn't beggar and rune the man she loved.

"Well, he took her at her word, but disbelieved and mocked at the raysons she gave—the omadhaun!

"He wasn't much good afther that, only for galloping his horse over the counthry like a madman, so I said to meself, says I, that we might as well take him with us into the Sleive-na-mon. I gave the ordhers, and there he is."

"Oh, the poor lad!" says Maureen; "does ould Bob suspect the boy is with the fairies?"

"Not in the laste," says the King. "You know how it is with us; whinever we take a person we lave one of our own in his place, who looks and acts and talks in a way that the presner's own mother can't tell the differ. By-and-by the fairy sickens and pretends to die, and has his wake and his burial. When the funeral's over he comes back to us hale and spiling for more sport. So the lad the O'Briens put into their tomb was one of our own—Phadrig Oge be name.

"Many a time Phadrig has taken the place of the genthry and quality in every county of Ireland, and has been buried more than a hundhred times, but he swears he never before had a dacinter funeral nor a rattliner wake."

"And the girl!" cried Maureen—"Norah, where is she?"

"Faith, that's strange, too," says the King. "She was the first person ould Bob axed for afther the funeral. He begged her to come back to them and forgive him, and the poor girl went agin to live at the big house."

"He'll get her another good husband yet," said Darby.

"Oh, never!" says Maureen, crying like a child. "She'll die of a broken heart."

"I've seen in me time," says the King, "people die from being pushed off houses, from falling in wells, and every manner of death you can mention, and I saw one ould woman die from ating too much treacle," he says, "but never a person die from a broken heart."

This he said to make light of what he had been telling, because he saw by Maureen's face that she was growing sick with pity. For Maureen was thinking of the black days when she herself was a prisoner in Sleive-na-mon.

For an answer to the jest, the girl, with her clasped hands held up to the King, moaned, "Oh, King, King, lave the poor lad go! lave him go. Take the black spell off him and send him home. I beg you lave him go!"

"Don't bother him," says Darby; "what right have we to interfere with the Good People?" Though at the same time he took the pipe from his mouth and looked kind of wistful at the little man.

But Maureen's tears only fell faster and faster.

"I can't do what you ask, avick," says the King, very kindly. "That day I let you and Darby go from us, the power to free anyone was taken away from me by my people. Now every fairy in Sleive-na-mon must give his consent before the spell can be taken away entirely from anyone; and, well, you know they'll never consent to that," he says.

"But what I can do, I will do. I can lift the spell from the omadhaun for one hour, and that hour must be just before cockcrow."

"Is that the law now?" asked Darby, curiously. Maureen was sobbing, so she couldn't speak.

"It is," says the Master of the Good People. "And tonight I'll sind our spy, Sheelah Maguire, to Norah Costello with the message that if Norah has love enough and courage enough in her heart to stand alone at her thrue lover's grave in Kilmartin churchyard, tomorrow night an hour before cockcrow, she'll see him plain and talk with him. And let you two be there," he says, "to know that I keep me word."

At that he vanished and they saw him no more that night, nor until two hours after the next midnight, when as they were tying the old horse and cart to the fence outside Kilmartin church, then they heard him singing. He was sitting on the wall, chanting at the top of his voice a strange, wild song, and holding in his hand a silver-covered noggin. On a fallen tombstone near by lay a white cloth, glimmering in the moonlight, and on the cloth was spread as fine a supper as heart could wish.

So beside the white rows of silent tombs, under the elm-trees and willows, they ate their fill, and Darby would have eaten more if close to them they hadn't heard a long, deep sigh, and caught a glimpse of a tall man, gliding like a shadow into the shadows that hung around the O'Briens' family vault.

At the same time, standing on the top of the stile which led into the graveyard, a woman's form was seen wavering in the moonlight.

They watched her coming down the walk betwixt the tombs, her hand on her breast, clutching tight the cloak. Now and then she'd stand, looking about the while, and shivering in mortal terror at the cry of the owls, and then she'd flit on and be lost in the shadows; and then they'd see her run out into the moonlight, where she'd wait again, gathering courage. At last she came to a strip of soft light before the tomb she knew. Her strength failed her there, and she went down on her knees.

Out of the darkness before her a low, pleading voice called, "Norah! Norah! Don't be frightened, acushla machree!"

Slowly, slowly, with its arm spread, the dim shape of a man glided out of the shadows. At the same instant the girl rose and gave one cry, as she flung herself on his breast. They could see him bending over her, then, pouring words like rain into her ears, but what he said they couldn't hear—Darby thinks he whispered.

"I wondher, oh, I wondher what he's telling her in this last hour!" says Maureen.

"It's aisy to know that," says Darby; "what should he be telling her but where the crocks of goold are hid."

"Don't be watching them, it ain't dacint," says the King; "uncultayvation or unpoliteness is ojus; come over here; I've a pack of cayrds, Darby," says he, "and as we have nearly an hour to wait, I challenge you to a game of forty-five."

"Sure we may as well," says Darby. "What can't be cured must be endured."

With that, my two bold heroes sat astride the fallen stone, and hammering the rock hard with their knuckles, played the game. Maureen went and, holding on to the ivy, knelt at the church wall—it's praying and crying, too, I think she was. Small blame to her if she was. All through that hour she imagined the wild promisings of the two poor creatures over by the tomb, and this kept burning the heart out of her.

Just as the first glow of gray broke behind the hills the King stood up and said: "It's your game, Darby, more be good luck than be good shooting; 'tis time to lave. You know if I'm caught out afther cockcrow I lose all me spells for the day, and besides I'm wisible to any mortal eye. I'm helpless as a baby then. So I think I'll take the omadhaun and go. The roosthers may crow now any minute," says he.

The omadhaun, although he couldn't hear, felt the charm drawing him. He threw a frightened look at the east and held the girl closer. 'Twas their last minute.

"King! King!" says Maureen, running up, "if I brought Sullivan's goat into Sleive-na-mon, would ye swear to let me out safe agin?"

"Troth, I would indade, I swear be Ould Nick!" ('Tis by him the Good People swear.) "I'll do that same."

"Then let the omadhaun go home. Get the Good People's consent and I'll bring you the goat," says Maureen.

The King trembled all over with anxiety and excitement. "Why didn't you spake sooner? I'm afeard I haven't time to go to Sleive-na-mon and back before cockcrow," he stuttered, "and at cockcrow, if the lad was undher the say or in the stars, that spell'd bring him to us, and then he could never agin come out till the Day of Judgement. Howsumever, I'll go and thry," he says, holding tight on to his crown with both hand; and with them words he vanished. By this and by that, it wasn't two minutes till he was back and with not a second to spare, either.

"Phadrig Oge wants Mrs. Nancy Clancy's nanny-goat, too. Will ye bring the both of them, Maureen?" he screamed.

"You're dhriving a hard bargain, King," cried Darby. "Don't promise him, Maureen."

"I will!" cried she.

"Then it's a bargain!" the fairy shouted, jumping to the top of a headstone. "We all consent," he says, waving the noggin.

He yelled to the omadhaun. "Go home, Roger O'Brien! Go back to your father's house and live your life out to its natural ind. The curse is lifted from you, the black spell is spint and gone. Pick up the girl, ye spalpeen; don't ye see she's fainted?"

When O'Brien looked up and saw the Master of the Fairies he staggered like a man that had been struck a powerful blow. Then he caught up the girl in his arms and ran with her down the gravelled path and over the stile.

At that minute the sorest misfortune that can happen to one of the Good People came to pass. As the lad left the churchyard every cock in the parish crowed, and, tare and hounds! There on a tombstone, caught by the cockcrow, stood the poor, frightened little King! His gold crown was far back on his head, and his green cloak was twisted behind his back. All the power for spells and charms was gone from him until the next sunset.

"I'm runed entirely, Darby!" he says. "Trow your shawl about me, Maureen alannah, and carry me in your arms, purtending I'm an infant. What'll I do at all at all?" says he, weakly.

Taking him at his word, Maureen wrapped the King in her shawl, and carrying him in her arms to the cart, laid him in the straw at the bottom, where he curled up, still and frightened, till they were on their way home.

Part II. The Couple Without Childher

Five miles down the road from Kilmartin churchyard, and then two miles across, lived Barney Casey with Judy, his wife—known far and wide as the Couple without Childher.

Some foolish people whispered that this lack of family was a punishment for an old secret crime. But that saying was nonsense, for a more honest couple the sun didn't shine on. It was only a penance sent from Heaven as any other penance is sent; 'twas—like poverty, sickness, or as being born a Connaught man—just to keep them humble-hearted.

But, oh, it was the sore penance!

Many an envious look they gave their neighbour, Tom Mulligan, the one-legged ballad-maker, who lived half a mile up the road, for twelve, pretty, red-haired innocents sported and fought before Tom's door. The couple took to going through the fields to avoid passing the house, for the sight of the children gave them the heartache.

By-and-by the two began conniving how unbeknownst they might buy a child, or beg or even steal one—they were that lonesome-hearted.

Howsomever, the plan at last they settled on was for Judy to slip away to a far part—Mayo, I think—where she would go through the alms-houses till she found a gossoon that suited her. And they had the cute plan laid by which it was to pass before the neighbours as their own—a Casey of the Caseys.

"Lave it to me, Barney darling," said Judy, with tears in her eyes, "and if the neighbours wondher where I am, tell them I've gone to spind a few months with my ould mother," says she.

Well, Judy stole off sly enough, and 'twas well until the cold weather when Barney got word that she had found a perfect angel, that it was the picture of himself, and that she would be home in a few days.

With a mind like thistle-down he ran to Father Scanlan to arrange for the christening. On his way to the priest's house he invited the first woman he met, Ann Mulligan, the ballad-maker's wife, to be godmother; he picked bashful Ted Murphy, the bachelor, to be godfather; and on his way home he was that excited and elated that he also invited big Mrs. Brophy, the proud woman, to be the boy's godmother, forgetting altogether there was such a person in the world as Ann Mulligan. The next day the neighbours made ready a great bonfire to celebrate the dispositious occasion.

But ochone! Midnight before the day of the christening poor Judy came home with empty arms and a breaking heart. The little lad had died suddenly and was buried. Maybe the Good People had taken him—'twas hard to tell which.

Tare and ages, there was the trouble! For two hours the couple sat in their desolate kitchen holding hands and crying and bawling together till Barney could stand it no longer. Snatching his caubeen, he fled from the coming disgrace and exposure out into the fields, where he wandered aimless till after dawn, stamping his feet at times and wagging his head, or shaking his fist at the stars.

At that same unlucky hour who should be jolting in their cart along the high-road, two miles across, on their way home from Kilmartin churchyard, but our three heroes, Maureen, the King, and Darby O'Gill!

Their old white horse bobbed up and down through the sticky morning fog, Darby and Maureen shivering on the front seat. The Ruler of the Fairies, Maureen's shawl folded about him, was lying cuddled below in the straw. When they saw anyone coming, the fairy-chief would climb into Maureen's lap, and she'd hold him as though he were a baby.

Small blame to him to be sour and sullen!

"Here I am," he says to himself, "his Majesty, Brian Connors, King of all the Good People in Ireland, the Master of the Night Time, and having been King for more than five thousand years, with more power after sunset than the Emperor of Greeze or the Grand Turkey of barbayrious parts—here am I," he says, "disguised as a baby, wrapped in a woman's shawl, and depending for my safety on two simple counthry people—" Then he groaned aloud, "Bad luck to the day I first saw the omadhaun!"

Those were the first words he spoke. But it wasn't in the little man to stay long ill-natured. At the first shebeen house that they found open, Maureen bought for him a bottle of spirits, and this cheered him greatly. The first drink warmed him, the second softened him, the third put a tune to the end of his tongue, and by the time they reached Tom Grogan's public-house, which was straight two miles across from Barney Casey's, the liquor set him singing like a nightingale.

Maureen and Darby slipped into Grogan's for a bit of warmth and a mouthful to eat, leaving the Master of Slieve-na-mon well wrapped up at the bottom of the cart—his head on a sack of oats and his feet against the cart-side—and as I said, him singing.

He had the finest, liftingest way for a ballad you ever heard! At the end of every verse he elevated the last word and held it high, and put a lonesome wobble into his voice that would make you cry.

Peggy Collins, the tall, thieving old beggar-woman who used to wear the dirty red cloak, and looked like a soldier in it, was sleeping inside the hedge as the cart came along; but when it stopped she peeped out to see who had the good song with him.

When she saw it was an infant not much longer than your two hands, "God presarve us and save us!" she gasped, and began to say her prayers. The King went on singing, clear and doleful and beautiful, the ballad of Donnelly and Cooper.

"Come all ye thrue-born Irishmen wherever you may be,
 I hope you'll pay attintion and listen unto me-e-e,
 And if you'll pay attintion the truth I will declare
 How Donnelly fought Cooper on the Curragh of Kildare."

Prayers were never from Peggy's heart, so as she listened to the entrancing song she turned from praying to plotting.

"If I had that child," she says, "I could go from fair to fair and from pathron to pathron, and his singing'd fill my apron with silver."

The King turned to another ditty, and you'd think he was a thrush.

"They'll kiss you, they'll car-r-ress you," he sang.
"They'll spind your money free,
 But of all the towns in Ire-eland Kilkenny for me-e-e-e."

The gray-haired old rascal, Peggy, by this was creeping ever and ever till she reached the cart. Up then she popped, and the first thing my poor Captain knew the shawl was slapped fast on his face, and two long, thin arms were dragging him out over the wheel. He tried to cry out, but the shawl choked him, and scrambling and kicking did him no good.

Over the nearest stile bounced Peggy, and into the nearest field she flew, her petticoat lifted, her white hair streaming, and her red cloak fluttering behind. She crunched the chief man of the fairies under her left elbow, his head banging behind, with as little reverence as if, saving your presence, he were a stray gander.

Well, your honour, Peggy ran till there wasn't a breath in her before she slowed down to a walk, and then she flung the King over her right shoulder, his face on her back in that way some careless women carry children. This set his head free.

When he saw who it was had stolen him, oh, but he was vexed; for all that he didn't say a word as they went, but lay there on her collar-bone, bobbing up and down, blinking his eyes, and thinking what he should do to her. At last he quietly reached over with his teeth and took a bite at the back of her neck that she felt to her toes. Wow! Your honour should have heard the screech Peggy let out of her!

Well, as she gave that screech she gave a jerk at the King's legs, pulling him down. As he flopped into her arms he took a wisp of her hair with him. For a second's time the spiteful little eyes in the old wizened face, looking up at her own from under the gold crown, froze her stiff with terror, and then, giving a yell that was ten times louder than the first screech, she flung his Majesty from her down upon the hard ground. Leaping a ditch, she went galloping wildly across the meadow. The King fell flat on his back with an unreasonable jolt.

That wasn't the worst of his bad luck. If Peggy had dropped him at any other place in the field he might have crawled off into the ditch and hid till sunset, but oh, asthore, there not ten rods away, with eyes bulging and mouth gaping, stood Barney Casey, the Man without Childher!

Barney looked from the little bundle on the ground to Peggy as she went skimming, like a big red bird, over the low-lying morning fog. Through his surprise a fine hope slowly dawned for him.

He said: "Good fortune folly you, and my blessing rest on you wherever you go, Peggy Bawn, for the throuble you've lifted this day; you've given me a Moses in the bull rushers or a Pharyoah's daughter, but I disremember which, God forgive me for forgetting my rayligion!"

He stood for a minute slyly looking to the north and the south and the east and the west. But what he saw, when he turned to look again for the baby, would have made any other man than one in Barney Casey's mind say his prayers and go on his way.

The baby was gone, but in its place was a little old man with a gold crown on his head, a silver-covered noggin in his hand, and the most vexed expression in the world on his face, and he trailing a shawl and trotting toward the ditch.

'Twas a hard fall for the Man without Childher, and hard he took it.

When Barney was done with bad language, he says, "A second ago, me ould lad, you were, or you pretended to be, an innocent child. Well, then, you'll turn back again every hair and every look of you; you'll be a smiling, harmless, purty baby agin, or I'll know the rayson why," he says, gritting his teeth.

With that he crept over and scooped up the King. There was the struggling and wiggling!

"Lave me down! Lave me down! You murthering spalpeen!" shouted the King, kicking vicious at Barney's chest. "I'm Brian Connors, the King of the Good People, and I'll make you sup sorrow in taycups for this!" cries he.

Well, Casey, his lips shut tight and his eyes grim and cold, held in his two hands, out at arm's-length, the little man, who was kicking furious. For a minute Barney studied him.

"I believe in my sowl," says the Man without Childher, mighty reproachful, "you're only a fairy! But if that's what you are, you must have charms and spells. Now turn yourself into a purty, harmless infant this minute—have red hair, like the Mulligan childher at that—or I'll break every bone in your body!"

There was blazing anger in the King's eye and withering scorn in his voice.

"Ignorant man," he cried, "don't you know that betwixt cockcrow in the morning and sunset the Good People can work no spell or charm. If you don't lave me down I'll have a mark on you and on all your relaytions the world'll wondher at!"

But the devil a bit frightened was Casey.

He started in to help the charm along as one would try to make a watch go. He shook the King slowly from side to side, then joggled him softly up and down, muttering earnestly betwixt his teeth, "Go on, now, you little haythen, change this minute, you scorpion of the world; come, come, twisht yourself!"

What the little King was saying all this time you must guess at, for I'm not bitter-tongued enough to repeat it.

Seeing that not a hair changed for all his work, Barney wrapped Maureen's shawl about the King and started for home, saying: "Hould your whist! It's a child I must have to be baptised this day. It'll be hard to manage, but I have a plan! You came as a child, and you'll be thrated as such—and look, if you don't quit kicking me in the stomach, I'll strangle you!"

As you know, to say pious words to one of the Good People is worse than cutting him with a knife, to show him pious pictures is like burning him, but to baptise a fairy is the most terrible punishment in the whole world.

As they went along, the King argued, besought and threatened, but he talked to stone.

At last, although he had but the strength of a six-year-old child, the Captain of the Good People showed what high spirit was in him.

"Set me down, you thief," he says. "I challenge you! If you have a dhrop of your mother's blood in you, set me ferninst you with sticks in our hands, so we can fight it out like men!"

"No, it's not needful," says Barney, cool as ice; "but in a few minutes I'll shave every hair from your head, and afther that make a fine Christian out of you. It's glad and thankful for it you ought to be, you wicious, ugly little pagan scoundhrel!"

Well, the King let a roar out of him: "You bandy-legged villain!" he cried—and then whirled in to abuse the Man without Childher. He insulted him in English, he jeered him in Irish, he traduced him in Latin and Russian, but the most awful crash of blackguarding that was known in Ireland since the world began was when the King used Chinese.

Casey looked wonder and admiration, but made no answer till the little man was out of breath, when he spoke up like a judge.

"Well, if there's any crather within the earth's four corners that needs baptising it's you, little man. But I'll not thrajooce you any more, for you're me own little Romulus or Raymus," he says scratching his head. Then of a sudden he broke out excitedly, "Now may four kinds of bad luck fall on your proud head this day, Mrs. Brophy, and four times heavier ones on you, Ann Mulligan, and may the curse of Cromwell light on you now and forever, Ted Murphy, the bachelor, for pushing yerselves here at this early hour in the morning!"

For the sight that met his eyes knocked every plan out of his head.

Long before the time she was expected, sailing down the road to his own house, happy and slow, came Ann Mulligan, carrying in her arms her two-weeks-old baby, Patsy Mulligan. With motion like a two-masted schooner, tacking in her pride from side to side, up the road came big Mrs. Brophy, the proud woman, carrying her little Cornaylius; behind Mrs. Brophy marched bashful Ted Murphy, the bachelor, his hands behind his back, his head bent like a captive, but stepping high. Not with the sheep-stealing air men are used to wear at christenings and weddings did Ted Murphy hop along, but with the look on his face of a man who had just been tried, convicted, sentenced, and who expects in a few minutes to be hung for sheep-stealing.

They were come an hour before the time to bring the child to the church.

Beside the door stood Judy, straining her eyes to know what Barney had hiding in the bundle, and with an awful fear in her heart that he had robbed some near neighbour's cradle.

Well, Barney at once broke into a run so as to get inside the house with the King, and to close the door before the others got there, but as luck would have it, the whole party met upon the threshold and crowded in with him.

"Oh, the little darling; give us a sight of the poor crachure," says Mrs. Mulligan, laying Patsy on the bed.

"He's mine first, if you plaze," says Mrs. Brophy, the proud woman.

"He's sick," says Barney—"too sick to be uncovered."

"Is he too sick to go to church?" broke in Ted Murphy, eagerly, hoping to get rid of his job.

"He is," says Barney, catching at a chance for delay.

"Then," says Ted, with joy in his voice, "I'll run and bring Father Scanlan to the house. I'll be back with him in tunty minutes," says he.

Before anyone could stop the gawk, he was flying down the road to the village. Casey felt his bundle shiver.

"I'll have your life's blood for this!" the King whispered, as Barney laid him on the bed betwixt the two children.

"Come out! come out!" cries Casey, spreading his arms and pushing the three women over the threshold before they knew it.

Then he stood outside, holding the door shut against the three women, trying to think of a plan, and listening to more blistering talk than he ever heard on any day before that day, for the three women talked at the same time, each striving to be more disagreeable than the other. What drove him crazy was that his own wife, Judy, was the worst. They threatened him, they wheedled, and they stormed. The priest might ride up at any minute. The sweat rained from Barney's forehead.

Once in desperation he opened the door to let the women pass, but shut it quick when he saw the King standing up on the bed and him changing his own clothes for those of little Patsy Mulligan.

Well, the women coaxed till Mrs. Mulligan lost all patience and went and sat sullen on the bench. At that Mrs. Brophy suddenly caught Barney around the waist, and whirling him aside, she and Judy rushed in. Barney, with the fierceness of a tiger, swung shut the door to keep Mrs. Mulligan at bay.

The other women inside were hopping with joy. Dressed in Maureen's shawl, but devil a thing else, lay on the outside edge of the bed poor little Patsy Mulligan. The King, almost smothered, dressed in Patsy's clothes, was scrooged in to the wall with a cloth about his head wrapped round and round.

"Oh, the little jewel," says Mrs. Brophy, picking up little Patsy Mulligan, and setting herself on the bed; "he's the dead cut of his father."

In that queer way women have, Judy already had half a feeling that the child by some kind of magic was her own. So she spoke up sharp and said that the child was the image of her brother Mike.

While they were disputing, Mrs. Brophy turned her head and saw the legs of the King below the edge of little Patsy's dress—the dress that he'd stole and put on.

"For the love of God, Mrs. Casey!" says she, laying her hand on Judy's shoulder, "did you ever before see feet on a child of two weeks old like them on Patsy Mulligan?"

Well, at this they laughed and tittered and doubled backward and forward on the bed, sniggering at the King and saying funny things about him, till, mad with the shame of the women looking at his bare knees, and stung by the provoking things they said, he did a very foolish thing;—he took a pin from his clothes and gave Mrs. Brophy so cruel a prod that, big as she was, and proud as she was, it lifted her in three leaps across the floor. "Whoop! whoop!" she says, as she was going. Now, though heavy and haughty, Mrs. Brophy was pretty nimble on her feet, for, red and indignant, she whirled in a twinkling. "Judy Casey," says she, glowering and squaring off, "if that's your ideeh of a good, funny joke, I'll taiche you a betther!" she says.

When Barney, outside listening with his heart in his mouth, heard the angry voices within, a great weakness came into his chest, for he thought everything was over. Mrs. Mulligan pushed past him—he lost the power to prevent her—and he followed her into the house with quaking knees. There was the uproar!

While the three were persuading the furious Mrs. Brophy that it must have been a pin in the bedclothes, Ted Murphy, breathless, flung open the door.

"Father Scanlan wants to know," he cried, "what ails the baby that you can't bring it to church," he says.

All turned questioning eyes to Barney, till his mind fluttered like a wounded partridge. Only two diseases could the unfortunate man on the sudden remember.

"It's half maysles and a thrifle of scarlet fever," he says. He couldn't easily have said anything worse. Seeing a terrible look on Mrs. Mulligan's face, he says again, "But I don't think it's ketching, ma'am."

The fright was on. With a great cry, Mrs. Brophy dived for and picked up little Cornaylius and rushed with him out of the door and down the road; Mrs. Mulligan, thinking she had little Patsy, because of the clothes, snatched up the King—his head still rolled in the cloth—and darted up the road. She was clucking curses like an angry hen as she went, and hugging the King and coddling him, and crying over him and saying foolish baby language, till he was so disgusted that he determined to give her a shock.

"Oh, me poor little darling!" she sobbed, pressing the King's head to her bosom—"oh, Patsy, me jewel, have they kilt you entirely?"

At that the King spoke up in a clear, cold voice.

Misdoubting her ears, Mrs. Mulligan stopped and bent her head, listening to her baby.

"Don't worry for me, ma'am, thank you kindly," says the baby, polite and strong. "Don't throuble yourself about the general state of my robustness," it says, "it's thraymendous," says the child—"in fact, I never was betther."

As cautiously as if she was unwrapping a roll of butter Mrs. Mulligan began to unwind the cloth from about the King's head.

When this was done she flung up her face and yelled, "Ow! ow! ow!" and then came right up from the ground the second hard jolt the King got that day.

As he lay on his back fastening his strange clothes and thinking what he would do next, he could hear Mrs. Mulligan going down the road. She was making a noise something like a steam whistle.

"Be-gorr," says the King, sitting up and feeling of his back, "to-day, with the women, I'm playing the divil entirely!"

Part III. The Luck of the Mulligans

The wee King of the Fairies sat in the dust of the road where Ann Mulligan had dropped him. There were dents in his gold crown, and the baby's dress he still wore was soiled and tore.

Ow! Ow! Ow! What a terrible jolt against the ground Ann Mulligan gave him when she took the covering from his head and found his own face gazing up at her instead of her baby Patsy's. He turned to shake his fist up the road, and twisted once more to shake his fist down the road.

"Be the bones of Pether White," he says, "what me and me subjects'll do to-night to this parish'll make the big wind seem like a cock's breath!

"But," he says, again, "how'll I hide meself till dark? Wirra! Wirra! if it were only sunset—the sun has melted every power and charm and and spell out of me—the power has left me four bones. I can be seen and molested by any spalpeen that comes along; what'll I do at all at all! I think I had best be getting through the fields back to Barney Casey's. It's little welcome they have for me there, but they must keep me saycret now for their own sakes."

With that he got upon his legs, and holding up his white dress, climbed through the stile into Casey's field.

The first thing he saw there was a thin but jolly-minded looking pig, pushing up roots with her nose and tossing them into the air through sheer devilment.

Dark-eyed Susan was she called, and she belonged to Tom Mulligan, the one-legged ballad-maker, who had named her after the famous ballad.

Mulligan was too tender-hearted to sell her to be killed, and too poor to keep her in victuals, so she roamed the fields, a shameless marauder and a nimble-footed freebooter.

"Be-gorr, here's luck!" said the little King; "since 'tis in Casey's field, this must be Casey's baste. I couldn't ask betther; whinever a pig is frightened it runs to its own house; so I'll just get on her back and ride down to Casey's cabin."

The King looked inquiring at Susan, and Susan looked impudent suspicion at the King.

"Oh, ho, ye beauty, you know what's in me mind!" says he, whistling and coaxing and sidling up to her. A pig likes a compliment if it's well told, so Susan hung her head, grunted coquettish, and looked away. Taking advantage of her head being turned, without another word, his Royal Highness ran over, laid hold of her ear, and with one graceful jump took an easy saddle-seat on her back.

This was the last thing the pig expected, so with one frightened squeal from Susan both of them were off like the wind through the fields toward Mulligan's house, taking stones, ridges, and ditches like hurdle jumpers till they came in sight of a mud-plastered cabin which stood on the hillside. A second after, the King's hair stood straight up and his heart grew cold, for there, sitting on the threshold, with her family in a little crowd about her, was the woman who, misconstruing him for her own child, had fled with him from Barney Casey's, and finding her mistake, had thrown him into the high-road.

About the ballad-maker's door was gathered his whole family, listening to the wonderful tale being told by Ann Mulligan. A frightened woman she was.

Indeed, when Ann Mulligan, after dropping the King in the road, reached home, she fell unconscionable in the door before her husband and her frightened children, and she never came to till little Pether sprinkled a noggin of water on her; then she opened her eyes and began telling how Old Nick had stolen the baby and had taken little Patsy's place in her own two arms.

There she sat wringing her hands and waving back and forth. The fairy-man could easily guess the story she was telling, and his flying steed was hurrying straight toward the house and nothing could stop it. They'd both be there in ten seconds.

"Well, this time, anyhow, I'll be kilt intirely," says the King.

Mrs. Mulligan turned to point down the road to the place where she had dropped the King, when, lo and behold, up the boreen and through the field they saw, coming at a tremendous pace, Dark-eyed Susan and the King, riding her like a dragoon.

Mrs. Mulligan gave one screech and, lifting her petticoats, flew; the children scurried off after her like young rabbits.

Tom, not being able to run because of his wooden leg, stood his ground, but at the same time, remembering more prayers and repenting of more mean things he'd done than ever before since he was born.

He was sure it was Old Nick himself that was in it.

And now a new danger jumped suddenly before the King. The pig headed for her favourite hole through the hedge, and when the King saw the size of the hole he let a howl out of him, for he knew he'd be thrown. He scrooched close to the beast's back and drew up his legs. Sure enough he was slithered off her back and left sitting on the hard ground, half the clothes torn from his royal back.

That howl finished Tom entirely, so that when his Majesty crawled through the hole after the pig and came over to him, the ballad-maker wouldn't have given tuppence for his soul's salvation. Howsomever, he put on the best and friendliest face he could under the circumstances. Scraping with his wooden leg and pulling at a tuft of carroty hair on his forehead, Tom said, mighty wheedling: "The top o' the day to your Honour. Sure, how's Mrs. Balzebub and the childher. I hear it's a fine, bright family your Lordship has. Arrah, it isn't the likes of me, poor Tom Mulligan, the ballad-maker, that your riverence'd be wanting."

Hearing them words, the King looked mighty pleased. "If you're Tom Mulligan, the ballad-maker," he says, coming over smiling, "it's proud and happy I am to meet you! I'm no less than Brian Connors, the King of the Good People," he says, drawing himself up and trying to look grand. "It's many's the fine ballad of yours we sing in Sleive-na-mon."

"But little Patsy," stammered Tom; "sure your Majesty wouldn't take him from us; he's our twelfth and rounds out the dozen, you know."

"Have no fear," says the fairy; "Patsy'll be here safe and sound at nightfall. If you stand friend to me this day the divil a friend you'll ever need agin as long as you live!" With that the King up and told him all the day's happenings and misfortunes. Tom could hardly believe his eyes or ears. He was so happy he began in his mind making a ballad about himself and the King that minute.

"Ow!" says the King, bending his back and holding his head, "whin I think of the ondacencies I wint true this day!"

"Your Majesty'll go through no more," says Tom. With that he went stumping away to call back the wife and children.

In a few minutes the ruler of the night-time was sitting on Mulligan's table eating the last petatie and drinking the last sip of new milk that was in the house. The King drained the cup and smacked his lips. "Now sing us a ballad, Tom Mulligan, my lad," says he, leaning back against the empty milkcrock and crossing his legs like a tailor. Ann Mulligan nodded, approving from where she sat, proud and contented on the bed; the children smiled up from the mud floor. So Tom, who was a most melodious man, just as his wife was a most harmonious woman, up and sang the ballad of Hugh Reynolds:

> "Me name is Hugh Reynolds, I came of dacint parents;
>   I was born in County Cavin, as you may plainly see.
> Be lovin' of a maid named Catherine McCabe,
>   My love has been bethrayed, she's a sore loss to me."

There's most of the time thirty-two verses to that song, and Tom sang them all without skipping a word.

"Bate that, King Brian Connors," he says at last. "I challenge you!"

Then King Brian threw back his head and, shutting his eyes, sang another ballad of forty-seven verses, which was Catherine McCabe's answer to Hugh Reynolds, and which begins this away:

> "Come all ye purty fair maids wherever you may
>   be,
> And if you'll pay attention and listen unto me,
> I'll tell of a desayver that you may beware of the
>   same,
> He comes from the town of Drumscullen in the
>   County Cavan, an' Hugh Reynolds is his name."

One song brought out another finer than the first, until the whole family, children and all, joined in singing, "Willie Reilly and His Dear Colleen Bawn."

'Twould make your heart young again to hear them. At the end of each verse all the Mulligans'd stop quick to let the King wobble his voice alone. Dark-eyed Susan was standing scratching herself inside the closed door, pleased but wondering; so, with sweet songs and old tales, the hours flew like minutes till at last the ballad-maker pushed back the table and tuned his fiddle, while the whole family—at least all of them old enough to stand—smiling, faced one another for a dance.

The King chose Mrs. Ann Mulligan for a partner. The fiddle struck a note, the bare, nimble feet raised. "Rocky Roads to Dublin" was the tune.

"Deedle, deedle, dee; deedle, deedle, diddle um.
Deedle, deedle, dee, rocky roads to Dubalin."

The twinkling feet fell together. Smiles and laughter and jostling and jollity broke like a summer storm through the room. And singing and pattering and jiggering, rose and swirled to the mad music, till suddenly—"knock, knock, knock!"—the blows of a whip-handle fell upon the door and every leg stopped stiff.

"Murther in Irish," whispered little Mickey Mulligan, "'tis Father Scanlan himself that's in it!"

Ochone mavrone! What a change from merry-making and happiness to fright and scandalation was there! The Master of the Fairies, sure that Father Scanlan had the scent of him, tried to climb up on to the settle-bed, but was too weak from fear, so Mrs. Mulligan hoisted him and piled three children on top of the King to hide him just as Father Scanlan pushed open the door.

The priest stood outside, holding his horse with one hand and pointing his whip with the other. "What are you hiding on that bed, you vagabone?" he says.

"Whist!" says Tom Mulligan, hobbling over and going outside, with the fiddle under his arm, "'tis little Patsy, the baby, and he ain't dressed dacint enough for your riverence to see," whispered the villain.

"Tom Mulligan," says the priest, shaking his whip, "you're an idle, shiftless, thriftless man, and a cryin' shame and a disgrace to my flock; if you had two legs I'd bate you within an inch of your life!" he says, looking stern at the fiddler.

"Faith, and it's sorry I am now for my other leg," says Tom, "for it's well I know that whin your riverence scolds and berates a man you only give him half a shilling or so, but if you bate him as well, your riverence sometimes empties your pockets to him."

'Twas hard for the priest to keep an ill-natured face, so he smiled; but as he did, without knowing it, he let fly a shot that brought terror to the heart of the ballad-maker. "God help me with you and the likes of you," says the priest, trying to look severe; "you keep me from morning till night robbing Pether to pay Paul. Barney Casey, the honest man, gives me a crown for baptising his child, and tin minutes afther I must give that same money to a blaggard!"

Well, when Mulligan heard that his own little Patsy had been baptised again at the instigation of that audacious impostor, Barney Casey, the ballad-maker's neck swelled with rage. But worse was to come. Gulping a great lump down his throat he asked: "What name did your riverence give the baby?" There was a tremble in the poor man's voice.

"Bonyface," says the priest, his toe in the stirrup. "Today is the feast of St. Bonyface, a gr-r-reat bishop. He was a German man," says Father Scanlan.

The groan Tom Mulligan let out of him was heartrending. "Bonyface! Oh, my poor little Patsy; bad scran to you, Barney Casey! My own child turned into a German man—oh, Bonyface!"

The priest was too busy mounting his horse to hear what the ballad-maker said, but just before starting the good man turned in his saddle. "I came near forgetting my errant," he says. "There's a little ould man—dwarves they call the likes of thim—

who has been lost from some thravelling show or carawan, or was stole by ould Peggy Collins this morning from some place—I don't rightly know which. Sind the childher looking for him and use him kind. I'm going up the road spreading the news. Ignorant people might misthrate him," says his reverence, moving off.

"You'll find no ignorant person up this road," called Tom, in a broken voice, "but Felix O'Shaughnessy, and he's not so bad, only he don't belave in ghosts," cried Mulligan.

Even as the ballad-maker turned to go in the door, the sun, shooting one red, angry look at the world, dropped below the western mountains. The King jumped from the bed.

"The charms have come back to me. I feel in my four bones the power, for 'tis sunset. I'm a greater man now than any king on his trone," says he. "Do you sind word to Barney and Judy Casey that if they don't bring little Patsy and my green velvet cloak and the silver-topped noggin and stand fernist me on this floor within half an hour, I'll have the both of thim presners in Sleive-na-mon before midnight, to walk on all-fours the rest of their lives. As for you, my rayspected people," he says, "a pleasanter afthernoon I seldom spint, and be ready to get your reward."

With those words, he vanished. Their surprise at his disappearance was no sooner over than the Mulligans began hunting vessels in which to put the gold the fairy was going to give them.

Ann Mulligan was dragging in from outside an empty tub when shamefaced Judy Casey passed in, carrying little Patsy Mulligan. Behind her slunk Barney, her husband, holding the green cloak and the silver-topped noggin.

"I had him for one day, Ann Mulligan," says Judy, handing little Patsy to his mother, "and though it breaks my poor, withered heart to give him up, he's yours by right, and here he is."

Whilst she was speaking those words the ruler of the fairies sprung over the threshold and laid a white bundle on the table. The household crowded up close around.

Without a word the fairy drew the cover from the white bundle, and there, like a sweet, pink rose, lay sleeping on its white pillow the prettiest baby you ever set your two living eyes on.

Judy gave a great gasp, for it was the identical child the fairies stole from her down in the County Mayo.

"You don't desarve much from me," says the King, "but because Ann Mulligan—fine woman—asked it, I'll do you a favour. You may take back the baby or I'll give you a hundhred pounds. Take your choice, Barney Casey."

Barney stood a long time with bowed head, looking at the child and thinking hard. You can surely see what a serious question he had. One's own child is worth more than a hundred pounds, but other people's children are plenty and full of failings. Mulligan's family peered up into his face, and his wife Judy searched him with hungry eyes. At last he said, very slow: "My mind has changed," says he. "Though people always tould me that childher were a throuble, a worry and a care, yesterday I'd give the County Clare for that little one. After this day's work I know that sayin's thrue, so I'll take the hundhred pounds," he says.

"Divil a fear of you takin' the hundhred pounds!" snapped his wife, Judy, grabbing up the child. And then the two women, turning on him, fell to abusing and ballyragging the Man without Childher, till sorra bit of courage was left in his heart.

"I promised you yer choice, and they'll lave you no choice," says the King, looking vexed. "Well, here's the hundhred pounds, and let Judy keep the child."

When the fairy turned to the ballad-maker, the hearts of all the Mulligans stopped still.

"Now, my grand fellow, me one-legged jaynious," he says, "you're going to be disappinted. You think I'll give you riches, but I won't." At that Tom's jaw dropped to his chest, and the littlest Mulligans began to cry.

"I'll not make you rich bekase you're a born ballad-maker, and a weaver of fine tales, and a jaynious—if you make a jaynious rich you take all the songs out of him and you spile him. A man's heart sthrings must be often stretched almost to the breaking to get good music from him. I'll not spile you, Tom Mulligan.

"Besides," he says, "as you are a natural-born ballad-maker, you'd kill yourself the first year thryin' to spind all your money at wanst. But I'll do betther for you than to make you rich. Ann Mulligan, do you clear the table an' put my silver-topped noggin on the edge of it," says he.

When Ann Mulligan did as she was bid, the king put the green cloak on his shoulders and, raising his hand, pointed to the silver-covered noggin. Everyone grew still and frightened.

"Noggin, noggin, where's your manners?" he says, very solemn.

At the last word the silver lid flew open, and out of the cup hopped two little men dressed all in black, dragging something after them that began to grow and grow amazing. So quickly did they work, and so swiftly did this thing they brought twirl and change and turn into different articles that the people hadn't time to mark what form it was at first, only they saw grow before their astonished eyes, teacups and dishes and great bowls, and things like that.

In a minute the table was laid with a white cloth like the quality have, and china dishes and knives and forks.

"Noggin, noggin, where's your manners?" says the King again. The little men dragged from the noggin other things that grew into a roast of mutton and boiled turnips, and white bread and butter, and petaties, and pots of tea.

"Noggin, noggin, where's your manners?" says the King, for the last time.

At that the little black men, after putting a silver shilling beside every plate at the table, jumped into the noggin and pulled down its lid.

When the eating and drinking and jollity were at their height, the King arose, drew tight his crown on his head, and pointing once more to the silver-covered noggin, said: "This is my gift to you and your reward, Tom Mulligan, maker of ballads and journeyman worker in fine tales. 'Tis more than your wish was. Nayther you nor anyone who sits at your table, through all your life, will ever want a bite to ate or a sup to dhrink, nor yet a silver shilling to cheer him on his way. Good luck to all here and good-bye!" Even as they looked at the King he was gone, vanished like a light that's blown out—and they never saw him more.

But the news spread. Musicianers, poets, and story-tellers, and geniuses flocked to the ballad-maker's cabin from all over Ireland. Any fine day in the year one might see them gather in a dozen knots before his door and into as many little crowds about the stable. In each crowd, from morning till night, there was a tune being played, a ballad sung, or a story being told. Always one could find there blacksmiths, schoolmasters, and tinkers, and all trades, but the greater number by far, of course, were beggarmen.

Nor is that same to be wondered at, because every genius, if he had his own way and could follow his own heart's desire, would start tomorrow at daybreak with the beggarman's staff and bag.

But wherever they came from, and whatever their station, Tom Mulligan stumped on his wooden leg from crowd to crowd, the jovial, happy master of them all.

SIX

The Banshee's Comb

Part I. The Diplomacy of Bridget

Twas the mending of clothes that All Souls' afternoon in Elizabaeth Ann Egan's kitchen that naturally brought up the subject of husbands and the best ways to manage them. And if there's one thing more than another that makes me take my hat off to the women, 'tis the audacious way the most down-trodden of their sex will brag about her blackguard husband.

Not that either one or the other of the five busy-tongued and busy-fingered neighbour women who bent above their sewing or knitting that afternoon were down-trodden; by no manner of means; far, far from it. They were so filled with matrimonial contentedness that they fairly trampled down one another to be first in praising the wonderful men of their choice. Every woman proudly claimed to own and control the handsomest, likeliest man that ever trod in brogues.

They talked so fast and they talked so loud that 'twas a trying long while before meek-voiced little Margit Doyle could squeeze her husband, Dan'l John, sideways into the argument. And even when she did get him to the fore, the other women had appropriated all the heroic qualifications for their own men, so that there was nothing left for Dan'l but the common leavings; and that deprivation nettled Margit and vexed her sore. But she took her chance when it came, poor as it was, and bolted in.

Jabbing the air as though her needle were a dagger, she broke into the disourse. "I wouldn't thrade my Dan for the King of Rooshia or the Imperor of Chiney," says she, peering defiant around the room. No one sided with that remark, and no one argued against it, and this vexed her the more.

"The Kingdom of Chiney is where the most supharior tay comes from," says Caycelia Crow. She was a large, solemn woman, was Mistress Crow, and a great historian.

"No," says Margit, scorning the interruptions, "not if the two men were rolled into one," says she.

"Why," says Caycelia Crow, and her deep voice tolled like a passing bell—"why," says she, "should any dacint woman be wantin' to marry one of thim haythen Imperors? Sure they're all ambiguious," she says, looking around, proud of the grand word.

Elizabeth Ann stopped the spinning-wheel the better to listen, while the others turned bothered faces to the historian.

"Ambiguious," says Mistress Crow, raising her voice in the middle part of the word; "ambiguious," she says again, "manes that accordin' to the laygal laws of some furrin parts, a man may marry four or five wives if he has a mind to."

At this Margit bristled up like a bantam-hen. "Do you mane to say, Caycelia Crow," says she, dropping in her lap the weskit she was mending, "do you intind to substantiate that I'm wishin' to marry the Imperor of Chiney, or," she says, her voice growing high and cutting as an east wind, "do you wish to inferentiate that if my Dan'l had the lave he'd be ambiguious? Will you plaze tell these friends and neighbours," she says, waving a hand, "which of the two of us you was minded to insinuate against?"

The attack was so sudden and so unexpected that Mistress Crow was too bewildered to defend herself. The poor woman only sat staring stupid at Margit.

The others sank back in their chairs speechless with consternation till Mollie Scanlan, wishing to pacify the situation, and winking friendly at Caycelia, spoke up soothering. "Thrue for ye, Margit Doyle," says she. "What kind of talk is that for ye to be talkin', Caycelia?" says she. "Sure if Dan'l John were to be med the Imperor of Chiney tomorrow he'd hesitate an' dayliberate a long time before bringin' in one of them ambiguious women to you an' the childher. I'd like to see him thry it. It'ud be a sore an' a sorrowful day for him, I'm thinkin'."

At them words, Margit, in her mind's eye, saw Dan'l John standing ferninst her with an ambiguious heathen woman on each side of him, and the picture riled the blood in her heart. "Oh, ho!" says she, turning on poor shrinking Mollie with a smile, and that same smile had loaded guns and pistols in it. "An' will you plaze be so kind an' condesinden', Misthress Scanlan," says she, "to explain what you ever saw or heerd tell of in my Dan'l John's actions, that'ud make you think he'd contimplate such schoundrel endayvours," says she, trembling.

The only answer to the question was from the tea-kettle. It was singing high and impudent on the hob.

Now, Bridget O'Gill, knowing woman that she was, had wisely kept out of the discourse. She sat apart, calmly knitting one of Darby's winter stockings. As she listened, howsomever, she couldn't keep back a sly smile that lifted one corner of her mouth.

"Isn't it a poor an' a pittiful case," said Mistress Doyle, glaring savage from one to the other, "that a dacint man, the father of noine childher, eight of them livin', an' one gone for a sojer—isn't it a burnin' shame," she says, whimpering, "that such a daycint man must have his char-ack-ther thrajuiced before his own wife— Will you be so good as to tell me what you're laughing at, Bridget O'Gill, ma'am?" she blazed.

Bridget, fluttering guiltly, tried to hide the misfortunate smile, but 'twas too late.

"Bekase, if it is my husband you're mocking at," says Margit, "let me tell you, fair an' plain, his ayquils don't live in the County of Tipperary, let alone this parish! 'Tis thrue," she says, tossing her head, "he hasn't spint six months with the Good People—he knows nothin' of fairies—but he has more sinse than those that have. At any rate, he isn't afeard of ghosts like a knowledgeable man that I could mintion."

That last thrust touched a sore spot in the heart of Bridget. Although Darby O'Gill would fight a dozen living men, if needful, 'twas well known he had an unreasonable fear of ghosts. So, Bridget said never a word, but her brown eyes began to sparkle, and her red lips were drawn up to the size of a button.

Margit saw how hard she'd hit, and she went on triumphant. "My Dan'l John'ud sleep in a churchyard. He's done it," says she, crowing.

Bridget could hold in no longer. "I'd be sore an' sorry," she says, "if a husband of mine were druv to do such a thing as that for the sake of a little pace and quiet," says she, turning her shoulder.

Tare and hounds, but that was the stroke! "The Lord bless us!" muttered Mollie Scanlan. Margit's mind went up in the air and stayed there whirling, whilst she herself sat gasping and panting for a reply. 'Twas a thrilling, suspenseful minute.

The china shepherd and shepherdess on the mantel stopped ogling their eyes and looked shocked at each other; at the same time Bob, the linnet, in his wooden cage at the door, quit his singing and cocked his head the better to listen; the surprised tea-kettle gave a gasp and a gurgle, and spluttered over the fire. In the terrible silence Elizabeth Egan got up to wet the tea. Setting the teapot in the fender she spoke, and she spoke resentful. "Any sinsible man is afeard of ghosts," says she.

"Oh, indade," says Margit, catching her breath. "Is that so? Well, sinsible or onsinsible," says she, "this will be Halloween, an' there's not a man in the parish who would walk past the churchyard up to Cormac McCarthy's house, where the Banshee keened last night, except my Dan'l!" says she, triumphant.

The hurt pride in Bridget rose at that and forced from her angry lips a foolish promise. "Huh! we hear ducks talkin'," she says, coolly rolling up Darby's stocking, and sticking the needle in the ball of yarn. "This afthernoon I was at Cormac McCarthy's," she says, "an' there wasn't a bit of tay in the house for poor Eileen, so I promised Cormac I'd send him up a handful. Now, be the same token, I promise you my Darby will make no bones of going on that errant this night."

"Ho! ho! ho!" laughed Margit. "If he has the courage to do it bid him sthop in to me on his way back, an' I'll send to you a fine settin' of eggs from my black Spanish hin."

What sharp word Mistress O'Gill would have flung back in answer no one knows, because when once provoked she has few equals for sarcastic language, but just then Elizabeth Ann put in Bridget's hand a steaming cup of good, strong tea. Now, whisky, ale, and porter are all good enough in their places, your honour—I've nothing to intimidate against them—but for a comforting, soothering, edifying beverage, give me a cup of fine black tea. So this day the cups were filled only the second time, when the subject of husbands was completely dropped, and the conversation wandered to the misdemeanors of Anthony Sullivan's goat.

All this time the women had been so busy with their talking and argufying that the creeping darkness of a coming storm had stolen unnoticed into the room, making the fire glow brighter and redder on the hearth. A faint flare of lightning, followed by a low grumble of thunder, brought the women to their feet.

"Marcy on us!" says Caycelia Crow, glad of an excuse to be gone, "do you hear that? We'll all be dhrownded before we raich home," says she.

In a minute the visitors, after draining their cups, were out in the road, each hurrying on her separate way, and tying her bonnet-strings as she went.

'Twas a heavy and a guilty heart that Bridget carried home with her through the gathering storm. Although Darby was an intimate friend of the fairies, yet, as Margit Doyle said, he had such a black dread of all other kinds of ghosts that to get him out on this threatening Halloween night, to walk past the churchyard, as he must do on his way to Cormac McCarthy's cottage, was a job equal to lifting the Shannon bridge. How she was to manage it she couldn't for the life of her tell; but if the errand was left undone she would be the laughing-stock of every woman in the parish.

But worst of all, and what cut her heart the sorest, was that she had turned an act of neighbourly kindness into a vainglorious boast; and that, she doubted not, was a mortal sin.

She had promised Cormac in the afternoon that as soon as she got home she would send Darby over with some tea for poor little Eileen, and now a big storm was gathering, and before she could have supper ready, try as hard as she could, black night might be upon them.

"To bring aise to the dying is the comfortingist privilege a man or woman can have, an' I've thraded it for a miserable settin' of eggs," she says. "Amn't I the unfortunit crachure," she thought, "to have let me pride rune me this away. What'll I do at all at all?" she cried. "Bad luck to the thought that took me out of me way to Elizabeth Egan's house!"

Then she made a wish that she might be able to get home in time to send Darby on his errand before the night came on. "If they laugh at me, that'll be my punishment, an' maybe it'll clane my sin," says she.

But the wish was in vain. For just as she crossed the stile to her own field the sun dropped behind the hills as though he had been shot, and the east wind swept up, carrying with it a sky full of black clouds and rain.

     *   *   *   *   *   *   *

That same All Souls' night Darby O'Gill, the friend of the fairies, sat, as he had often sat before, amidst the dancing shadows, ferninst his own crackling turf and wood fire, listening to the storm beat against his cottage windows. Little Mickey, his six-year-old, cuddled asleep on his daddy's lap, whilst Bridget sat beside them, the other children cradled around her. My, oh my, how the rain powered and hammered and swirled!

Out in the highway the big drops smashed against wayfarers' faces like blows from a fist, and once in a while, over the flooded moors and the far row of lonesome hills, the sullen lightning spurted red and angry, like the vicious flare of a volcano.

You may well say 'twas perfect weather for Halloween—tonight when the spirits of the departed dead visit once again their homes, and sit unseen, listening and yearning about the old hearthstones.

More than once that evening Darby'd shivered and shuddered at the wild shrieks and wails that swept over the chimney-tops; he being certain sure that it wasn't the wind at all, but despairing voices that cried out to him from the cold lips of the dead.

At last, after one particular doleful cry that rose and fell and lingered around the roof, the knowledgeable man raised his head and fetched a deep breath, and said to his wife Bridget: "Do you hear that cry, avourneen? The dear Lord be marciful to the souls of the dayparted!" sighed he.

Bridget turned a troubled face toward him. "Amen," she says, speaking softly; "and may He preserve them who are dying this night. Poor Eileen McCarthy—an' she the purty, light-footed colleen only married the few months! Haven't we the raysons to be thankful and grateful. We can never pray enough, Darby," says she.

Now the family had just got off their knees from night prayers, that had lasted half an hour, so them last words worried Darby greatly.

"That woman," he says to himself, mighty sour, "is this minute contimplaytin' an' insinuatin' that we haven't said prayers enough for Eileen, when as it is, me two poor knees have blisters on thim as big as hin's eggs from kneelin'. An' if I don't look out," he says to himself again, "she'll put the childher to bed and then she's down on her knees for another hour, and me wid her; I'd never advise anyone to marry such a pious woman. I'm fairly kilt with rayligion, so I am. I must disthract her mind an' prevent her intintions," he says to himself.

"Maybe, Bridget," he says, out loud, as he was readying his pipe, "it ain't so bad afther all for Eileen. If we keep hoping for the best, we'll chate the worst out of few good hours at any rate," says the knowledgeable man.

But Bridget only rolled the apron about her folded arms and shook her head sorrowful at the fire. Darby squinted carefully down the stem of his pipe, blew in it, took a sly glance at his wife, and went on: "Don't you raymember, Bridget," he says, "whin ould Mrs. Rafferty lay sick of a bad informaytion of the stomick; well, the banshee sat for a full hour keening an' cryin' before their house—just as it did last night outside Cormac McCarthy's. An' you know the banshee cried but once at Rafferty's, but never rayturned the second time. The informaytion left Julia, and all the wide worruld knows, even the King of Spain might know if he'd sent to ax, that Julia Rafferty, as strong as a horse, was diggin' petaties in her own field as late as yesterday."

"The banshee comes three nights before anyone dies, doesn't it, daddy?" says little Mickey, waking up, all excited.

"It does that," says Darby, smiling proud at the child's knowledgeableness; "and it's come but once to Eileen McCarthy."

"An' while the banshee cries, she sits combing her hair with a comb of goold, don't she, daddy?"

Bridget sat uneasy, biting her lips. Always and ever she had strove to keep from the children tidings of fairies and of banshees and ghosts and other unnatural people. Twice she threw a warning look at Darby, but he, not noticing, went on, stroking the little lad's hair, and saying to him: "It does, indade, avick; an' as she came but once to Mrs. Rafferty's, so we have rayson to hope she'll come no more to Cormac McCarthy's."

"Hush that nonsinse!" says Bridget, looking daggers; "sure Jack Doolan says that 'twas no banshee at all that come to Rafferty's, but only himself who had taken a drop too much at the fair, an' on his way home sat down to rest himself by Rafferty's door. He says that he stharted singin' pious hymns to kape off the evil spirits, and everyone knows that the same Jack Doolan has as turrible a woice for singin' as any banshee that ever twishted a lip," she says.

The woman's contrariness vexed Darby so he pounded his knee with his fist as he answered her: "You'll not deny, maybe," he says, "that the Costa Bower sthopped one night at the Hall, and—"

"Whist!" cried Bridget; "lave off," she says; "sure that's no kind of talk to be talkin' this night before the childher," says she.

"But mammy, I know what the Costa Bower is," cried little Mickey, sitting up straight in Darby's lap and pointing his finger at his mother; "'tis I that knows well. The Costa Bower is a gr-r-reat black coach that comes in the night to carry down to Croaghmah the dead people the banshee keened for."

The other children by now were sitting bolt upright, stiff as ramrods, and staring wild-eyed at Mickey.

"The coachman's head is cut off an' he houlds the reins this away," says the child, letting his hands fall limp and open at his side. "Sometimes it's all wisable, an' then agin it's unwisable, but always whin it comes one can hear the turrible rumble of its wheels." Mickey's voice fell and, spreading out his hands, he spoke slow and solemn. "One Halloween night in the woods down at the black pond, Danny Hogan heard it coming an' jumped behind a stone. The threes couldn't sthop it, they wint right through it, an' as it passed, Danny Hogan says he saw one white, dead face laned back agin the dark cushions, an' this is the night—All Sowls' night—whin it's sure to be out; now don't I know?" he says, triumphant.

At that Bridget started to her feet. For a minute she stood speechless with vexation at the wild, frightening notions that had got into the heads of her children; then "Glory be!" she says, looking hard at Darby. You could have heard a pin drop in the room. Old Malachi, the big yellow cat, who until this time lay coiled asleep on a stool, was the best judge of Bridget's character in that house. So, no sooner did he hear the words and see Bridget start up, then he was on his own four feet, his back arched, his tail straight up, and his two golden eyes searching her face. One look was enough for him. The next instant he leapt to the ground and started for the far room. As he scampered through the door, he threw a swift look back at his comrades, the children, and that look said plain as any words could say: "Run for it while you've time! Folly me; some one of us vagabones has done something murtherin'!"

Malachi was right; there would have been serious trouble for all hands, only that a softening thought was on Bridget that night which sobered her temper. She stopped a bit, the frown on her face clearing as she looked at the children, and she only said: "Come out of this! To bed with yez! I'm raising a pack of owdacious young romancers, an' I didn't know it. Mickey sthop that whimpering an' make haste with your clothes. The Lord help us, he's broke off another button. Look at that, now!" she says.

There was no help for them. So, with longing looks thrown back at their father, sitting cozy before the fire, and with consoling winks and nods from him, the children followed their mother to the bedroom.

Then, whilst Bridget was tucking the covers about them, and hushing their complainings, Darby sat with his elbows on his knees, doing in his head a sum in figures; and that sum was this: "How much would it be worth this All Sowls' night for a man to go out that door and walk past the churchyard up to Cormac McCarthy, the stone-cutter's house?" One time he made the answer as low as ten pounds two shillings and tuppence, but as he did so a particular loud blast went shrieking past outside, and he raised the answer to one thousand five hundred and twenty pounds sterling. "And cheap at that," he said aloud.

While he was studying these sagacious questions, Bridget stole quietly behind and put a light hand on his shoulder. For a minute, then, neither of them said a word.

Surprised at the silence, and puzzled that little Mickey had escaped a larruping, Malachi crept from the far room and stood still in the doorway, judging his mistress. An expression was on her face the cat couldn't quite make out. 'Twas an elevated, pitying, good-hearted, determined look, such as a man wears when he goes into the sty to kill one of his own pigs for Christmas.

Malachi, being a wise and experienced beast, decided to take no chances, so he backed through the door again and hid under the dresser to listen.

"I was just thinking, Darby avourneen," says the woman, half whispering, "how we might this blessed night earn great credit for our two souls."

"Wait!" says the sly man, straightening himself, and raising a hand. "The very thing you're going to spake was in my own mind. I was just dayliberatin' that I hadn't done justice tonight to poor Eileen. I haven't said me prayers farvint enough. I niver can whin we're praying together, or whin I'm kneeling down. Thin, like every way else, there's something quare about me. The foinest prayers I ever say is whin I'm be myself alone in the fields," says the conniving villain. "So, do you, Bridget, go in an' kneel down by the childher for a half hour or so, an' I'll sit here doing my best. If you should happen to look out at me ye might aisily think," he says, "that I was only sittin' here comfortably smoking my pipe, but at the same time prayers'll be whirlin' inside of me like a wind-mill," says he.

"Oh, thin, ain't I glad an' happy to hear you say thim worruds," says his wife, putting one fine arm about his neck; "you've taken a load off my heart that's been weighing heavy on it all night, for I thought maybe you'd be afeard."

"Afeard of what?" axed Darby, lifting his eyebrows. Malachi trotted boldly in and jumped up on the stool.

"You know Father Cassidy says," whispered Bridget, "that a loving deed of the hands done for the disthressed is itself a prayer worth a week of common prayers."

"I have nothin' agin that sayin'," says Darby, his head cocked, and he growing suspicious.

Bridget wiped her forehead with her apron. "Well, this afthernoon I was at McCarthy's house," she went on, soothering his hair with one hand, "an', oh, but the poor child was disthressed! Her cheeks were flaming with the faver. An', Darby, the thirst, the awful thirst! I looked about for a pinch of tay—there's nothing so coolin' for one in the faver as a cup of wake tay—an' the sorra scrap of it was in the house, so I tould Cormac that tonight, as soon as the childher were in bed, I'd send you over with a pinch."

Every one of Darby's four bones stiffened and a mortal chill struck into his heart.

"Listen, darlint," she says, "the storm's dying down, so while you're putting on your greatcoat I"ll wrap up the bit of tay."

He shook her hand from his shoulders. "Woman," he says, with bitter politeness, "I think you said that we had a great chanst to get credit for our two sowls. That's what I think you reymarked and stibulated," says he.

"Arrah, shouldn't a woman have great praise an' credit who'll send her husband out on such a night as this," his wife says. "The worse the conditions, the more credit she'll get. If a ghost were to jump at ye as you go past the churchyard, oughtn't I be the happy woman entirely?" says Bridget.

There was a kind of a tinkle in her voice, such as comes when Bridget is telling jokes, so Darby, with a sudden hope in his mind, turned quick to look at her. But there she stood grim, unfeeling, and determined as a pointed gun.

"Oh, ho! Is that the way it is?" he says. "Well, here's luck an' good fortune to the ghost or skellington that lays his hand on me this blessed night!" He stuck his two hands deep in his pockets and whirled one leg across the other—the most aggravating thing a man can do.

But Bridget was not the least discouraged; she only made up her mind to come at him on his soft side, so she spoke up and said: "Suppose I was dying of the faver, Darby O'Gill, an' Cormac rayfused to bring over a pinch of tay to me. What, then, would ye think of the stone-cutter?"

Malachi, the cat, stopped licking his paws, and threw a sharp, inquiring eye at his master.

"Bridget," says the knowledgeable man, giving his hand an argufying wave. "We have two separate ways of being good. Your way is to scurry round an' do good acts. My way is to keep from doing bad ones. An' who knows," he says, with a pious sigh, "which way is the betther one. It isn't for us to judge," says he, shaking his head solemn at the fire.

Bridget walked out in front of him and folded her arms tight. "So you won't go," she says sharp and sudden.

"The divil a foot!" says he, beginning to whistle.

You'd think, now, Bridget was beat, but she still held her trump card, and until that was played and lost the lad wasn't safe. "All right, me brave hayro," says she; "do you sit there be the fire; I'll go meself," she says. With that she bounced into the children's room and began to get ready her cloak and hood.

For a minute Darby sat poking the fire, muttering to himself and feeling very discommodious. Then, just to show he wasn't the least bit uneasy, the lad cleared his throat, and wagging his head at the fire, began to sing.

> "Yarra! as I walked out one mor-r-nin' all in the month
>   of June
> The primrosies and daisies an' cowslips were in bloom,
> I spied a purty fair maid a-sthrollin' on the lea,
> An' Rory Bory Alice, nor any other ould ancient
>   haythan goddess, was not half so fair as she.
> Says I, 'Me purty fair maid, I'll take you for me bride,
> An' if you'll pay no at-TIN-tion —' "

Glancing up sudden, he saw Malachi's eye on him, and if ever the features of a cat spoke silent but plain language, Malachi's face talked that minute to its master, and this is what it said: "Well, of all the cowardly, creaking bostheens I ever see in all me born days you are the worst, Darby O'Gill. You've not only guve impidence to your wife—an' she's worth four of you—but you've gone back on the friends you purtended to—"

Malachi's features got no further in their insulting remarks, for at that Darby swooped up a big sod of turf and let it fly at the audacious beast.

Now it is well known that by a spontaneous throw like that no one ever yet hit a sensible cat, but always and ever in that unlucky endeavour he strikes a damaginger blow where it's not intended. So it was this time.

Bridget, wearing her red cloak and hood, was just coming through the door, and that misfortunate sod of turf caught her fair and square, right below the chest, and she staggered back against the wall.

Darby's consternation and complication and turpitation were beyond imagination.

Bridget leaned there gasping. If she felt as bad as she looked, four Dublin surgeons with their saws and knives couldn't have done her a ha-porth of good. Howsomever, for all that, the sly woman had seen Malachi dodge and go galloping away, but she pretended to think 'twas at herself the turf was thrown. Not that she scolded, or anything so common as that, but she went on like an early Christian martyr who was just going to be introduced to the roaring lions.

Well, as you may easily see, the poor man, her husband, hadn't a chance in the world after that. Of course, to rectify himself, he'd face all the ghosts in Croaghmah. So, in a minute, he was standing in his greatcoat with his hand on the latch. There was a packet of tea in his pocket, and he was a subdued and conquered man.

He looked so woeful that Bridget repented and almost relented.

"Raymember," he says, mournful, "if I'm caught this night be the Costa Bower, or be the banshee, take good care of the childher, an' raymember what I say—I didn't mane, Bridget, to hit ye with that sod of turf."

"Oh, ain't ye the foolish darlin' to be afeared," smiled Bridget back at him, but she was serious, too. "Don't you know that when one goes on an errant of marcy a score of God's white angels with swoords in their hands march before an' beside an' afther him, keeping his path free from danger?" With that she pulled his face down to hers, and kissed him as she used in the old courting days.

There's nothing puts so much high courage and clear, steadfast purpose in a man's heart, if it be properly given, as a kiss from the woman he loves. So, with the warmth of that kiss to cheer him, Darby set his face against the storm.

Part II. The Banshee's Halloween

Halloween night, to all unhappy ghosts, is about the same as St. Patrick's Day is to you or to me—'tis a great holiday in every churchyard. And no one knew this better or felt it keener than did Darby O'Gill, that same Halloween night, as he stood on his own doorstep with the paper of black tea for Eileen McCarthy safely stowed away in the crown of his top-hat.

No one in that barony was quicker than he at an act of neighbourly kindness, but now, as he huddled himself together in the shelter of his own eaves, and thought of the dangers before, and of the cheerful fire and comfortable bed he was leaving behind, black rebellion rushed shouting across his heart. "Oh, my, oh, my, what a perishin' night to turn a man out into!" he says. "It'd be half a comfort to know I was goin' to be kilt before I got back, just as a warnin' to Bridget," says he.

The mistreated lad turned a sour eye on the tumultuous weather, and groaned deep as he pulled closer about his shoulders the cape of his greatcoat and plunged into the deserted and flooded roadway.

Howsomever, 'twas not the pelting rain, nor the lashing wind, nor yet the pitchy darkness that bothered the heart out of him as he went splashing and stumbling along the road. A thought of something more relentless than the storm, more mysterious than the night's blackness put pounds of lead into the lad's unwilling brogues; for somewhere in the shrouding darkness

125

that covered McCarthy's house the banshee was waiting this minute, perhaps, ready to jump out at him as soon as he came near her.

And, oh, if the banshee nabbed him there, what in the world would the poor lad do to save himself?

At the realisation of this situation, the goose-flesh crept up his back and settled on his neck and shoulders. He began to cast about in his mind for a bit of cheer or a scrap of comfort, as a man in such circumstances will do. So, grumbling and sore-hearted, he turned over Bridget's parting words. "If one goes on an errant of marcy," Bridget had said, "a score of God's white angels with swoords in their hands march before an' beside an' afther him, keeping his path free from danger."

He felt anxious in his hat for the bit of charitable tea he was bringing, and was glad to find it there safe and dry enough, though the rest of him was drenched through and through.

"Isn't this an act of charity I'm doin', to be bringin' a cooling drink to a dyin' woman?" he asked himself aloud. "To be sure it is. Well, then, what rayson have I to be afeared?" says he, poking his two hands into his pockets. Arrah, it's easy enough to bolster up one's heart with wise sayings and heroic precepts when sitting commodious by one's own fire; but talking wise words to one's self is mighty poor comfort when you're on the lonely high-road of a Halloween night, with a churchyard waiting for you on the top of the hill not two hundred yards away. If there was only one star to break through the thick sky and shine for him, if there was but one friendly cow to low or a distant cock to break the teeming silence, 'twould put some heart into the man. But not a sound was there, only the swish and wailing of the wind through the invisible hedges.

"What's the matther with the whole worruld? Where is it wanished to?" says Darby. "If a ghost were to jump at me from the churchyard wall, where would I look for help? To run is no use," he says, "an' to face it is—"

Just then the current of his misdoubtings ran whack up against a saying of old Peggy O'Callaghan. Mrs. O'Callaghan's reputation for truth and veracity, when it came to fairy tales or ghost stories, be it known, was equal if not superior to the best in Tipperary. Now, Peggy had told Ned Mullin, and Ned Mullin had told Bill Donahue, the tinker, and the tinker had advised Darby that no one need ever be afraid of ghosts if he only had the courage to face them.

Peggy said, "The poor crachures ain't roamin' about shakin' chains an' moanin' an' groanin', just for the sport of scarin' people, nor yet out of maneness. 'Tis always a throuble that's on their minds—a message they want sent, a secret they're endayvouring to unload. So instead of flyin' from the onhappy things, as most people generally do," she said, "one should walk up bowld to the apparraytion, be it gentle or common, male or faymale, an' say, 'What throubles ye, sir?' or 'What's amiss with ye, ma'am?' An' take my worrud for it," says she, "ye'll find yourself a boneyfactor to them when you laste expect it," she says.

'Twas a queer idea, but not so unreasonable after all, when one comes to think of it; and the knowledgeable man fell to deliberating whether he'd have the hardness to follow it out if the chance came. Sometimes he thought he would, then again he was sure he wouldn't. For Darby O'Gill was one who bent quick under trouble like a young tree before a hurricane, but he only bent—the trouble never broke him. So, at times his courage went down to a spark like the light of a candle in a gust of wind, but before you could turn on your heel 'twas blazing up strong and fiercer than before.

While thus contemplating and meditating, his foot struck the bridge in the hollow just below the burying-ground, and there as the boy paused a minute, churning up bravery enough to carry him up the hill and past the mysterious gravestones, there came a short quiver of lightning, and in its sudden flare he was sure he saw not ten yards away, and coming down the hill toward him, a dim shape that took the breath out of his body.

"Oh, be the powers!" he gasped, his courage emptying out like water from a spilled pail.

It moved, a slow, grey, formless thing without a head, and so far as he was able to judge, it might be about the size of an elephant. The persecuted lad swung himself sideways in the road, one arm over his eyes and the other stretched out at full length, as if to ward off the terrible visitor.

The first thing that began to take any shape in his bewildered brain was Peggy O'Callaghan's advice. He tried to follow it out, but a chattering of teeth was the only sound he made. And all this time a tremendous splashing, like the flopping of whales, was coming nearer and nearer.

The splashing stopped not three feet away, and the haunted man felt in the spine of his back and in the calves of his legs that a powerful, unholy monster towered over him.

Why he didn't swoon in his tracks is the wonder. He says he would have dropped at last if it weren't for the distant bark of his own good dog, Sayser, that put a throb of courage into his bones. At that friendly sound he opened his two dry lips and stuttered this saying: "Whoever you are, an' whatever shape ye come in, take heed that I'm not afeared," he says. "I command ye to tell me your throubles an' I'll be your boneyfactor. Then go back dacint an' rayspectable where you're buried. Spake an' I'll listen," says he.

He waited for a reply, and getting none, a hot splinter of shame at being so badly frightened turned his soul into vexation. "Spake up," he says, "but come no furder, for if you do, be the hokey I'll take one thry at ye, ghost or no ghost!" he says. Once more he waited, and as he was lowering the arm from his eyes for a peek, the ghost spoke up, and its answer came in two pitiful, distressed roars. A damp breath puffed across his face, and opening his eyes, what should the lad see but the two drooping ears of Solomon, Mrs. Kilcannon's grey donkey. Five different kinds of disgust boiled up into Darby's throat and almost strangled him. "Ye murdherin', big-headed imposture!" he gasped.

Half a minute after, a brown hoot-owl, which was sheltered in a near-by blackthorn tree, called out to his brother's family which inhabited the belfry of the chapel above on the hill that some black-minded spalpeen had hold of Solomon Kilcannon by the two ears and was kicking the ribs out of him, and that the language the man was using to the poor beast was worse than scandalous.

Although Darby couldn't understand what the owl was saying, he was startled by the blood-curdling hoot, and that same hoot saved Solomon from any further extraordinary trouncing, because as the angry man stopped to hearken, there flashed on him the realisation that he was beating and cruel mistreating a blessing in disguise. For this same Solomon had the reputation of being the knowingest, sensiblist thing which walked on four legs in that parish. He was a favourite with young and old, especially with children, and Mrs. Kilcannon said she could talk to him as if he were a human, and she was sure he understood. In the face of those facts, the knowledgeable man changed his tune, and putting his arm friendly around the distressed animal's neck, he said: "Aren't ye ashamed of yerself, Solomon, to be payradin' and mayandherin' around the churchyard Halloween night, dishguisin' yerself this away as an outlandish ghost, an' you havin' the foine repitation for daciency an' good manners?" he says, excusing himself. "I'm ashamed of you, so I am, Solomon," says he, hauling the beast about in the road, and turning him till his head faced once more the hillside. "Come back with me now to Cormac McCarthy's, avourneen. We've each been in worse company, I'm thinkin'; at laste you have, Solomon," says he.

129

At that, kind and friendly enough, the forgiving beast turned with him, and the two keeping each other slithering company, went stumbling and scrambling up the hill toward the chapel. On the way Darby kept up a one-sided conversation about all manner of things, just so that the ring of a human voice, even if 'twas only his own, would take a bit of the cruel lonesomeness out of the dark hedges.

"Did you notice McDonald's sthrame as you came along the night, Solomon? It must be a roarin' torrent be this, with the pourin' rains, an' we'll have to cross it," says he. "We could go over McDonald's stone bridge that stands ferninst McCarthy's house, with only Nolan's meadow betwixt the two, but," says Darby, laying a hand, confidential on the ass's wet back, "'tis only a fortnit since long Faylix, the blind beggarman, fell from the same bridge and broke his neck, an' what more natural," he asked, "than that the ghost of Faylix would be celebraytin' its first Halloween, as a ghost, at the spot where he was kilt?"

You may believe me or believe me not, but at those words, Solomon stopped dead still in his tracks and refused to go another step till Darby coaxed him by saying: "Oh, thin, we won't cross it if you're afeared, little man," says he, "but we'll take the path through the fields on this side of it, and we'll cross the sthrame by McCarthy's own wooden foot-bridge. 'Tis within tunty feet of the house. Oh, ye needn't be afeared," he says again; "I've seen the cows cross it, so it'll surely hould the both of us."

A sudden remembrance whipped into his mind of how tall the stile was, leading into Nolan's meadow, and the boy was puzzling deep in his mind to know how was Solomon to climb across that stile, when all at once the gloomy western gate of the graveyard rose quick by their side.

The two shied to the opposite hedge, and no wonder they did.

Fifty ghosts, all in their shrouds, sat cheek by jowl along the churchyard wall, never caring a ha'-porth for the wind or the rain.

There was little Ted Rogers, the humpback, who was drowned in Mullin's well four years come Michaelmas; there was black Mulligan, the gamekeeper, who shot Ryan, the poacher, sitting with a gun on his lap, and he glowering; beside the gamekeeper sat the poacher, with a jagged black hole in his forehead; there was Thady Finnegan, the scholar, who was disappointed in love and died of a decline; further on sat Mrs. Houlihan, who departed this life from eating of poison mushrooms; next to her sat—oh, a hundred others!

Not that Darby saw them, do ye mind. He had too good sense to look that way at all. He walked with his head turned out to the open fields, and his eyes squeezed shut. But something in his mind told him they were there, and he felt in the marrow of his bones that if he gave them the encouragement of one glance, two or three'd slip off the wall and come moaning over to tell him their troubles.

What Solomon saw and what Solomon heard, as the two went shrinking along'll never be known to living man, but once he gave a jump, and twice Darby felt him trembling, and when they reached at last the chapel wall, the beast broke into a swift trot. Pretty soon he galloped, and Darby went galloping with him, till two yellow blurs of light across in a field to the left marked the windows of the stone-cutter's cottage.

'Twas a few steps only, then, to the stile over into Nolan's meadow, and there the two stopped, looking helpless at each other. Solomon had to be lifted, and there was the trouble. Three times Darby tried by main strength to hoist his companion up the steps, but in vain, and Solomon was clean disgusted.

Only for the tender corn on our hero's left little toe, I think maybe that at length and at last the pair would have got safe over. The kind-hearted lad had the donkey's two little hoofs planted on the top step, and whilst he himself was lifting the rest of the beast in his arms, Solomon got uneasy that he was going to be thrown, and so began to twist and squirm; of course, as he did, Darby slipped and went thump on his back against the stile, with Solomon sitting comfortable on top of the lad's chest. But that wasn't the worst of it, for as the beast scrambled up he planted one hard little hoof on Darby's left foot, and the knowledgeable man let a yowl out of him that must have frightened all the ghosts within miles.

Seeing he'd done wrong, Solomon bolted for the middle of the road and stood there wiry and attentive, listening to the names flung at him from where his late comrade sat on the lowest step of the stile nursing the hurt foot.

'Twas an excited owl in the belfry that this time spoke up and shouted to his brother down in the blackthorn: "Come up, come up quick!" it says. "Darby O'Gill is just afther calling Solomon Kilcannon a malayfactor."

Darby rose at last, and as he climbed over the stile he turned to shake his fist toward the middle of the road. "Bad luck to ye for a thick-headed, ongrateful informer!" he says; "you go your way an' I'll go mine—we're sundhers," says he. So saying, the crippled man went limping and grumbling down the boreen, through the meadow, whilst his deserted friend sent reproachful brays after him that would go to your heart.

The throbbing of our hero's toe banished all pity for the beast, and even all thoughts of the banshee, till a long, gurgling, swooping sound in front told him that his fears about the rise in McDonald's stream were under rather than over the actual conditions.

Fearing that the wooden foot-bridge might be swept away, as it had been the year previous, he hurried on.

Most times this stream was only a quiet little brook that ran betwixt pretty green banks, with hardly enough water in it to turn the broken wheel in Chartres' ruined mill; but tonight it swept along, an angry, snarling, growling river that overlept its banks and dragged wildly at the swaying willows.

By a narrow throw of light from McCarthy's side window, our traveller could see the maddened water striving and tearing to pull with it the props of the little foot-bridge; and the boards shook and the centre swayed under his feet as he passed over. "Bedad, I'll not cross this way goin' home, at any rate," he says, looking back at it.

The words were no sooner out of his mouth than there was a crack, and the middle of the foot-bridge lifted in the air, twisted round for a second, and then hurled itself into the stream, leaving the two ends still standing in their place on the banks.

"Tunder an' turf!" he cried, "I mustn't forget to tell the people within of this, for if ever there was a thrap set by evil spirits to drownd a poor, unwary mortial, there it stands. Oh, ain't the ghosts turrible wicious on Halloween!"

He stood dripping a minute on the threshold, listening; then, without knocking, lifted the latch and stepped softly into the house.

*　　*　　*　　*　　*　　*　　*

Two candles burned above the blue and white china dishes on the table, a bright fire blazed on the hearth, and over in the corner where the low bed was set, the stone-cutter was on his knees beside it.

Eileen lay on her side, her shining hair strealed out on the pillow. Her pretty, flushed face was turned to Cormac, who knelt with his forehead hid on the bedcovers. The colleen's two little hands were clasped about the great fist of her husband, and she was talking low, but so earnest that her whole life was in every word.

"God save all here!" said Darby, taking off his hat, but there was no answer. So deep were Cormac and Eileen in some conversation they were having together that they didn't hear his coming. The knowledgeable man didn't know what to do. He realised that a husband and wife about to part for ever were looking into each other's hearts, for maybe the last time. So he just stood shifting from one foot to the other, watching them, unable to depart, and not wishing to intrude.

"Oh, it isn't death at all that I fear," Eileen was saying. "No, no, Cormac asthore, 'tis not that I'm misdoubtful of; but, ochone mavrone, 'tis you I fear!"

The kneeling man gave one swift upward glance, and drew his face nearer to the sick wife. She went on, then, speaking tender and half smiling and stroking his hand: "I know, darlint, I know well, so you needn't tell me, that if I were to live with you a thousand years you'd never sthray in mind or thought to any other woman, but it's when I'm gone—when the lonesome avenings folly aich other through days an' months, an' maybe years, an' you sitting here at this fireside without one to speak to, an' you so handsome an' gran', an' with the penny or two we've put away—"

"Oh, asthore machree, why can't ye banish thim black thoughts!" says the stone-cutter. "Maybe," he says, " the banshee will not come again. Ain't all the counthry-side prayin' for ye this night, an' didn't Father Cassidy himself bid you to hope? The saints in Heaven couldn't be so crool!" says he.

But the colleen went on as though she hadn't heard him, or as if he hadn't interrupted her: "An' listen," says she; "they'll come urging ye, the neighbours, an' raysonin' with you. Your own flesh an' blood'll come, an', no doubt, me own with them, an' they all sthriving to push me out of your heart, an' to put another woman there in my place. I'll know it all, but I won't be able to call to you, Cormac machree, for I'll be lying silent undher the grass, or undher the snow up behind the church."

While she was saying them last words, although Darby's heart was melting for Eileen, his mind began running over the colleens of that townland to pick out the one who'd be most likely to marry Cormac in the end. You know how far-seeing and quickminded was the knowledgeable man. He settled sudden on the Hanlon girl, and decided at once that she'd have Cormac before the year was out. The indecency of such a thing made him furious at her.

He says to himself, half crying, "Why, then, bad cess to you for a shameless, red-haired, forward baggage, Bridget Hanlon, to be runnin' afther the man, an' throwing yourself in his way, an' Eileen not yet cold in her grave!" he says.

While he was saying them things to himself, McCarthy had been whispering fierce to his wife, but what it was the stone-cutter said, the friend of the fairies couldn't hear. Eileen herself spoke clear enough in answer, for the fever gave her unnatural strength.

"Don't think," she says, "that it's the first time this thought has come to me. Two months ago, whin I was sthrong an' well an' sittin' happy as a meadowlark at your side, the same black shadow dhrifted over me heart. The worst of it an' the hardest to bear of all is that they'll be in the right, for what good can I do for you when I'm undher the clay," says she. "It's different with a woman. If you were taken an' I left I'd wear your face in my heart through all me life, an' ax for no sweeter company."

"Eileen," says Cormac, lifting his hand, and his voice was hoarse as the roar of the sea, "I swear to you on me bendid knees—"

With her hand on his lips, she stopped him. "There'll come on ye by daygrees a great cravin' for sympathy, a hunger an' a longing for affection, an' you'll have only the shadow of my poor, wanished face to comfort you, an' a recollection of a woice that is gone for ever. A new, warm face'll keep pushin' itself betwixt us—"

"Bad luck to that red-headed hussy!" muttered Darby, looking around distressed. "I'll warn Father Cassidy of her an' of her intintions the day afther the funeral."

There was silence for a minute; Cormac, the poor lad, was sobbing like a child. By-and-by Eileen went on again, but her voice was failing and Darby could see that her cheeks were wet. "The day'll come when you'll give over," she says. "Ah, I see how it'll all ind. Afther that you'll visit the churchyard be stealth, so as not to make the other woman sore-hearted."

"My, oh, my, isn't she the far-seein' woman?" thought Darby.

"Little childher'll come," she says, "an' their soft, warm arrums will hould you away. By-and-by you'll not go where I'm laid at all, an' all thoughts of these few happy months we've spent together— Oh! Mother in Heaven, how happy they were—"

The girl started to her elbow, for, sharp and sudden, a wild, wailing cry just outside the window startled the shuddering darkness. 'Twas a long cry of terror and of grief, not shrill, but piercing as a knife-thrust. Every hair on Darby's head stood up and pricked him like a needle. 'Twas the banshee!

"Whist, listen!" says Eileen. "Oh, Cormac asthore, it's come for me again!" With that, stiff with terror, she buried herself under the pillows.

A second cry followed the first, only this time it was longer, and rose and swelled into a kind of a song that broke at last into the heart-breakingest moan that ever fell on mortal ears. "Ochone!" it sobbed.

The knowledgeable man, his blood turned to ice, his legs trembling like a hare's, stood looking in spite of himself at the black window-panes, expecting some frightful vision.

After that second cry the voice balanced itself up and down into the awful death keen. One word made the whole song, and that was the terrible word, "Forever!"

"Forever an' forever, oh, forever!" swung the wild keen, until all the deep meaning of the word burned itself into Darby's soul, then the heart-breaking sob, "Ochone!" ended the verse.

Darby was just wondering whether he himself wouldn't go mad with fright, when he gave a sudden jump at a hard, strained voice which spoke up at his very elbow.

"Darby O'Gill," it said, and it was the stone-cutter who spoke, "do you hear the death keen? It came last night; it'll come tomorrow night at this same hour, and then—oh, my God!"

Darby tried to answer, but he could only stare at the white, set face and the sunken eyes of the man before him.

There was, too, a kind of fierce quiet in the way McCarthy spoke that made Darby shiver.

The stone-cutter went on talking the same as though he was going to drive a bargain. "They say you're a knowledgeable man, Darby O'Gill," he says, "an' that once a time you spint six months with the fairies. Now I make you this fair, square offer," he says, laying a forefinger in the palm of the other hand. "I have fifty-three pounds that Father Cassidy's keeping for me. Fifty-three pounds," he says again. "An' I have this good bit of a farm that me father was born on, an' his father was born on, too, and the grandfather of him. An' I have the grass of seven cows. You know that. Well, I'll give it all to you, all, every stiver of it, if you'll only go outside an' dhrive away that cursed singer." He threw his head to one side and looked anxious up at Darby.

The knowledgeable man racked his brains for something to speak, but all he could say was, "I've brought a bit of tay from the wife, Cormac."

McCarthy took the tea with unfeeling hands, and went on talking in the same dull way. Only this time there came a hard lump in his throat now and then that he stopped to swallow.

"The three cows I have go, of course, with the farm," says he. "So does the pony an' the five pigs. I have a good plough an' a foine harrow; but you must lave my stone-cutting tools, so little Eileen an' I can earn our way wherever we go, an' it's little the crachure ates the best of times."

The man's eyes were dry and blazing; no doubt his mind was cracked with grief. There was a lump in Darby's throat, too, but for all that he spoke up scolding-like. "Arrah, talk rayson, man," he says, putting two hands on Cormac's shoulders; "If I had the wit or the art to banish the banshee, wouldn't I be happy to do it an' not a fardin' to pay?"

"Well, then," says Cormac, scowling, and pushing Darby to one side, "I'll face her myself—I'll face her an' choke that song in her throat if Sattin himself stood at her side."

With those words, and before Darby could stop him, the stone-cutter flung open the door and plunged out into the night. As he did so the song outside stopped. Suddenly a quick splashing of feet, hoarse cries, and shouts gave tidings of a chase. The half-crazed gossoon had started the banshee—of that there could be no manner of doubt. A remembrance of the awful things that she might do to his friend petrified the heart of Darby.

Even after these cries died away he stood listening a full minute, the soles of his two brogues glued to the floor. The only sounds he heard now were the deep ticking of a clock and a cricket that chirped slow and solemn on the hearth, and from somewhere outside came the sorrowful cry of a whippoorwill. All at once a thought of the broken bridge and of the black, treacherous waters caught him like the blow of a whip, and for a second drove from his mind even the fear of the banshee.

In that one second, and before he realised it, the lad was out under the dripping trees, and running for his life toward the broken foot-bridge. The night was whirling and beating above him like the flapping of tremendous wings, but as he ran Darby thought he heard, above the rush of the water and through the swish of the wind, Cormac's voice calling him.

The friend of the fairies stopped at the edge of the foot-bridge to listen. Although the storm had almost passed, a spiteful flare of lightning leapt up now and again out of the western hills, and after it came the dull rumble of distant thunder; the water splashed spiteful against the bank, and Darby saw that seven good feet of the bridge had been torn out of its centre, leaving uncovered that much of the black, deep flood.

He stood straining his eyes and ears in wonderation, for now the voice of Cormac sounded from the other side of the stream, and seemed to be floating toward him through the field over the path Darby himself had just travelled. At first he was mightily bewildered at what might bring Cormac on the other side of the brook, till all at once the murdering scheme of the banshee burst in his mind like a gunpowder explosion.

Her plan was as plain as day—she meant to drown the stone-cutter. She had led the poor, distracted man straight from his own door down to and over the new stone bridge, and was now deluding him on the other side of the stream, back again up the path that led to the broken foot-bridge.

In the glare of a sudden blinding flash from the middle of the sky, Darby saw a sight he'll never forget till the day he dies. Cormac, the stone-cutter, was running toward the death-trap, his bare head thrown back, and his two arms stretched out in front of him. A little above and just out of reach of them, plain and clear as Darby ever saw his wife Bridget, was the misty white figure of a woman. Her long, waving hair strealed back from her face, and her face was the face of the dead.

At the sight of her Darby tried to call out a warning, but the words fell back into his throat. Then again came the stifling darkness. He tried to run away, but his knees failed him, so he turned around to face the danger.

As he did so he could hear the splash of the man's feet in the soft mud. In less than a minute Cormac would be struggling in the water. At the thought, Darby, bracing himself body and soul, let a warning howl out of him.

"Hould where you are!" he shouted; "she wants to drown ye—the bridge is broke in the middle!" But he could tell, from the rushing footsteps and from the hoarse swelling curses which came nearer and nearer every second, that the deluded man, crazed with grief, was deaf and blind to everything but the figure that floated before his eyes.

At that hopeless instant Bridget's parting words popped into Darby's head. "When one goes on an errant of marcy, a score of God's white angels, with swoords in their hands, march before an' beside an' afther him, keeping his path free from danger."

How it all come to pass he could never rightly tell, for he was like a man in a dream, but he recollects well standing on the broken end of the bridge, Bridget's words ringing in his ears, the glistening black gulf beneath his feet, and he swinging his arms for a jump. Just one thought of herself and the children, as he gathered himself for a spring, and then he cleared the gap like a bird.

As his feet touched the other side of the gap, a terrific screech—not a screech, either, but an angry, frightened shriek—almost split his ears. He felt a rush of cold, dead air against his face, and caught a whiff of newly turned clay in his nostrils; something white stopped quick before him, and then, with a second shriek, it shot high in the darkness and disappeared. Darby had frightened the wits out of the banshee.

The instant after, the two men were clinched and rolling over and over each other, down the muddy bank, their legs splashing as far as the knees in the dangerous water, and McCarthy raining weak blows on the knowledgeable man's head and breast.

Darby felt himself going into the river. Bits of the bank caved under him, splashing into the current, and the lad's heart began clunking up and down like a churn-dash.

"Lave off, lave off!" he cried, as soon as he could catch his breath. "Do you take me for the banshee?" says he, giving a desperate lurch and rolling himself on top of the other.

"Who are you, then? If you're not a ghost, you're the divil, at any rate," gasped the stone-cutter.

"Bad luck to ye!" cried Darby, clasping both arms of the haunted man. "I'm no ghost, let lone the divil—I'm only your friend, Darby O'Gill."

Lying there, breathing hard, they stared into the faces of each other a little space till the poor stone-cutter began to cry. "Oh, is that you, Darby O'Gill? Where is the banshee? Oh, haven't I the bad fortune," he says, striving to raise himself.

"Rise up," says Darby, lifting the man to his feet and steadying him there. The stone-cutter stared about like one stunned by a blow.

"I don't know where the banshee flew, but do you go back to Eileen as soon as you can," says the friend of the fairies. "Not that way, man alive," he says, as Cormac started to climb the foot-bridge, "it's broke in the middle; go down an' cross the stone bridge. I'll be after you in a minute," he says.

Without a word, meek now and biddable as a child, Cormac turned, and Darby saw him hurry away into the blackness.

The reasons Darby remained behind were two: first and foremost, he was a bit vexed at the way his clothes were muddied and bedraggled, and himself had been pounded and hammered; and second, he wanted to think. He had a queer cold feeling in his mind that something was wrong—a kind of a foreboding, as one might say.

As he stood thinking, a realisation of the calamity struck him all at once like a rap on the jaw—he had lost his fine brier pipe. The lad groaned as he began the anxious search. He slapped furiously at his chest and side pockets, he dived into his trousers and greatcoat, and at last, sprawling on his hands and feet like a monkey, he groped savagely through the wet, sticky clay.

"This comes," says the poor lad, grumbling and groping, "of pokin' your nose into other people's business. Hallo, what's this?" says he, straightening himself. "'Tis a comb. Be the powers of Pether, 'tis the banshee's comb."

And so indeed it was. He had picked up a gold comb the length of your hand and almost the width of your two fingers. About an inch of one end was broken off, and dropped into Darby's palm. Without thinking, he put the broken bit into his weskit pocket, and raised the biggest half close to his eyes, the better to view it.

"May I never see sorrow," he says, "if the banshee mustn't have dropped her comb. Look at that, now. Folks do be sayin' that 'tis this gives her the foine singing voice, bekase the comb is enchanted," he says. "If that sayin' be thrue, it's the faymous lad I am from this night. I'll thravel from fair to fair, an' maybe at the ind they'll send me to parliament."

With these words he lifted his caubeen and stuck the comb in the top tuft of his hair.

Begor, he'd no sooner gave it a pull than a sour, singing feeling begun at the bottom of his stomach, and it rose higher and higher. When it reached his chest, he was just going to let a bawl out of himself, only that he caught sight of a thing fernist him that froze the marrow in his bones.

He gasped short and jerked the comb out of his hair, for there, not ten feet away, stood a dark, shadowy woman, tall, thin, and motionless, leaning on a crutch.

During a breath or two the persecuted hero lost his head completely, for he never doubted that the banshee had changed her suit of clothes to chase back after him.

The first clear emotion that returned to him was to fling the comb on the ground and make a bolt of it. On second thought he knew that 'twould be easier to beat the wind in a race than to run away from the banshee.

"Well, there's a good Tipperary man done for this time," groaned the knowledgeable man, "unless in some way I can beguile her." He was fishing in his mind for a civil word when the woman spoke up, and Darby's heart jumped with gladness as he recognised the cracked voice of Sheelah Maguire, the spy for the fairies.

"The top of the avenin' to you, Darby O'Gill," says Sheelah, peering at him from under her hood, the two eyes of her glowing like tallow candles; "amn't I kilt with astonishment to see you here alone this time of the night," says the old witch.

Now, the clever man knew as well as though he had been told, when Sheelah said them words, that the banshee had sent her to look for the comb, and his heart grew bold; but he answered her polite enough, "Why, thin, luck to ye, Misthress Maguire, ma'am," he says, bowing grand, "sure, if you're kilt with astonishment, amn't I sphlit with inkerdoolity to find yourself mayandherin' in this lonesome place on Halloween night."

Sheelah hobbled a step or two nearer, and whispered confidential. "I was wandherin' hereabouts only this morning," she says, "an' I lost from me hair a goold comb—one that I've had this forty years. Did ye see such a thing as that, agra?" And her two eyes blazed.

"Faix, I dunno," says Darby, putting his two arms behind him. "Was it about the length of yer hand an' the width of yer two fingers?" he asked.

"It was," says she, thrusting out a withered paw.

"Thin I didn't find it," says the tantalising man. "But maybe I did find something summillar, only 'twasn't yours at all, but the banshee's," he says, chuckling.

Whether the hag was intentioned to welt Darby with her staff, or whether she was only lifting it for to make a sign of enchantment in the air, will never be known, but whatever she meant, the hero doubled his fists and squared off; at that she lowered the stick, and broke into a shrill, cackling laugh.

"Ho, ho!" she laughed, holding her sides, "but aren't ye the bould, distinguishable man. Becourse 'tis the banshee's comb; how well ye knew it! Be the same token I'm sint to bring it away; so make haste to give it up, for she's hiding an' waiting for me down at Chartres' mill. Aren't you the courageous blaggard, to grabble at her, an' thry to ketch her. Sure, such a thing never happened before, since the worruld began," says Sheelah.

The idea that the banshee was hiding and afraid to face him was great news to the hero. But he only tossed his head and smiled superior as he made answer. "'Tis yourself that knows well, Sheelah Maguire, ma'am," answers back the proud man, slow and deliberate, "that whin one does a favour for an unearthly spirit he may daymand for pay the favours of three such wishes as the spirit has power to give. The worruld knows that. Now I'll take three good wishes, such as the banshee can bestow, or else I'll carry the goolden comb straight to Father Cassidy. The banshee hasn't goold nor wor'ly goods, as the sayin' is, but she has what suits me betther."

This cleverness angered the fairy-woman, so she set in to abuse and to frighten Darby. She ballyragged, she browbeat, she traduced, she threatened, but 'twas no use. The bold man held firm, till at last she promised him the favours of the three wishes.

"First an' foremost," says he, "I'll want her never to put her spell on me or any of my kith an' kin."

"That wish she gives you, that wish she grants you, though it'll go sore agin the grain," snarled Sheelah.

"Then," says Darby, "my second wish is that the black spell be taken from Eileen McCarthy."

Sheelah flustered about like an angry hen. "Wouldn't something else do as well?" she says.

"I'm not here to argify," says Darby, swinging back and forward on his toes.

"Bad scran to you," says Sheelah. "I'll have to go an' ask the banshee herself about that. Don't stir from that spot till I come back."

You may believe it or not, but with that saying she bent the head of her crutch well forward, and before Darby's very face she threw—saving your presence—one leg over the stick as though it had been a horse, and while one might say Jack Robinson, the crutch rose in the air and lifted her, and she went sailing out of sight.

Darby was still gaping and gawking at the darkness where she disappeared when—whisk! she was back again and dismounting at his side.

"The luck is with you," says she, spiteful. "That wish I give, that wish I grant you. You'll find seven crossed rushes undher McCarthy's door-step; uncross them, put them in fire or in wather, an' the spell is lifted. Be quick with the third wish— out with it!"

"I'm in a more particular hurry about that than you are," says Darby. "You must find me my brier pipe," says he.

"You omadhaun," sneered the fairy-woman, "'tis sthuck in the band of your hat, where you put it when you left your own house the night. No, no, not in front," she says, as Darby put up his hand to feel. "It's stuck in the back. Your caubeen's twishted," she says.

Whilst Darby was standing with the comb in one hand and the pipe in the other, smiling delighted, the comb was snatched from his fingers and he got a welt in the side of the head from the crutch. Looking up, he saw Sheelah twenty feet in the air, headed for Chartres' mill, and she cackling and screeching with laughter. Rubbing his sore head and muttering unpious words to himself, Darby started for the new bridge.

In less than no time after, he had found the seven crossed rushes under McCarthy's door-step, and had flung them into the stream. Then, without knocking, he pushed open McCarthy's door and tiptoed quietly in.

Cormac was kneeling beside the bed with his face buried in the pillows, as he was when Darby first saw him that night. But Eileen was sleeping as sound as a child, with a sweet smile on her lips. Heavy perspiration beaded her forehead, showing that the fever was broke.

Without disturbing either of them, our hero picked up the package of tea from the floor, put it on the dresser, and with a glad heart stole out of the house and closed the door softly behind him.

Turning toward Chartres' mill, he lifted his hat and bowed low. "Thank you kindly, Misthress Banshee," he says. "'Tis well for us all I found your comb this night. Public or private, I'll always say this for you—you're a woman of your worrud," he says.

Part III. The Ghosts at Chartres' Mill

For a little while after Darby O'Gill sent the banshee back her comb, there was the dickens to pay in that townland. Each night came stormier than the other. And the rain—never, since Noey the Phoenaycian hoisted sail for Arrayat was there promised such a denudering flood. (In one way or another we're all, even the German men and the Fardowns, descendants of the Phoenaycians.)

Even at that the foul weather was the last of the trouble—the country-side was haunted. Every ghost must have left Croaghmah as soon as twilight to wander abroad in the lonesome places. The farmyards and even the village itself was not safe.

One morning, just before cock-crow, big Joey Hooligan, the smith, woke up sudden, with a terrible feeling that some ghastly person was looking in at him through the window. Starting up flurried in bed, what did he see but two eyes that were like burning coals of fire, and they peering steady into the room. One glance was enough. Giving a tremendous gasp, Joey dropped back quaking into the bed, and covered his head with the bed-clothes. How long after that the two hideous eyes kept staring at the bed Joey can't rightly tell, for he never uncovered his head nor stirred hand nor foot again till his wife Nancy had lighted the fire and boiled the stirabout.

Indeed, it was a good month after that before Joey found courage enough to get up first in the morning so as to light the fire. And on that same memorable morning, he and Nancy lay in bed arguing about it till nearly noon—the poor man was that frightened.

The evening after Hooligan was visited, Mrs. Norah Clancy was in the stable milking her cow—Cornaylia by name—when sudden she spied a tall, strange man in a topcoat standing near the stable door and he with his back turned toward her. At first she thought it a shadow, but it appeared a trifle thicker than a shadow, so, a little afraid, she called out: "God save you kindly, sir!"

At that the shadow turned a dim, grey face toward her, so full of reproachful woe that Mrs. Clancy let a screech out of her and tumbled over with the pail of milk betwixt her knees. She lay on her back in the spilt milk, unconscionable for a full fifteen minutes.

The next night a very reliable tinker, named Bothered Bill Donahue, while wandering near Chartres' ruined mill, came quite accidental upon twenty skeletons, and they colloguing and confabbing together on the flat roof of the mill-shed.

But worst of all, and something that struck deeper terror into every heart, was the news that six different persons at six different places had met with the terrible phantom coach, the Costa Bower.

Peggy Collins, a wandering beggar woman from the west country, had a wild chase for it; and if she'd been a second later reaching the chapel steps and laying her hand on the church-door, it would have had her sure.

Things got on so that after dark people only ventured out in couples or in crowds, and in point of piety that parish was growing into an example and pattern for the nation.

But of all the persons whom them conditions complicated, you may be sure that the worst harried and implicated was the knowledgeable man, Darby O'Gill.

There was a weight on his mind, but he couldn't tell why, and a dread in his heart that had no reasonable foundation. He moped and he moothered. Some of the time he felt like singing doleful ballads and death keens, and the rest of the time he could hardly keep from crying. His appetite left him, but what confused him worse than all the rest was the fondness that had come over him for hard work—cutting turf and digging petaties, and things like that.

To make matters more unsociable, his friend, Brian Connors, the king of the Fairies, hadn't showed a nose inside Darby's door for more than a fortnight; so the knowledgeable man had no one to advise with.

In them dismal circumstances Darby, growing desperate, harnessed the pony, Clayopathra, one morning and drove up to Clonmel to see the Master Doctor—the renowned McNamara. By this you may know how bad he felt, for no one, till he was almost at the point of desolation, ever went to that crass, browbeating old codger.

So, loath enough was our own hero to face him, and hard-hearted enough was the welcome the crabbed little doctor held out to Darby when they met.

"What did you ate for breakwus?" the physician says, peering savage from under his great eyebrows at Darby's tongue.

"Only a bowl of stirabout, an' a couple of petaties, an' a bit of bacon, an' a few eggs." He was counting on his fingers, "an'—an' somethin' or other I forgot. Do you think I'll go into a daycline, Doctor, agra?"

"Hump! ugh! ugh!" was all the comfort the sick man got from the blinking old blackguard. But turning immediate to his medicine-table, the surgeon began studying the medicines. There was so much of it ferninst him he might have given a gallon and never missed it. There was one fine big red bottle in particular Darby had his eye on, and thought his dose would surely come out of that. But McNamara turns to a box the size of your hat, and it filled to the top with little, white, flat pills. Well, the stingy old rascal counts out three and, handing them to Darby, says: "Take one before breakwus, another before dinner, an' the last one before suppher, an' give me four silver shillings, an' that'll cure ye," he says.

You may be sure that Darby boiled up inside with madness at the unreasonableness of the price of the pills, but, holding himself in, he says, very cool and quiet: "Will you write me out a raycept for the money, Doctor McNamara, if you plaze?" he says. And, whilst the old cheater was turned to the writing, by the hokey if our hero didn't half fill his pockets with pills from the box. By means of them, as he drove along home, he was able to do a power of good to the neighbour people he met with on the road.

When you once get in the habit of it, there's no pleasure in life which equals giving other people medicine.

Darby generously made old Peggy O'Callaghan take six of the little round things. He gave a swallow to half-witted Red Durgan, and a good mouthful to poor sick Eileen McCarthy (only she had to gulp them whole, poor thing, and couldn't eat them as the others did—but maybe 'twas just as good). And he gave a fistful each to Judy Rafferty and Dennis Hogan; and he stood handsome treat to a stranger, who, the minute he got the taste well into his mouth, wanted to fight Darby. Howsomever, the two only called each other hard names for a while, then Darby joggled along, doing good and growing lighter-hearted and merrier-minded at every stop he made. 'Twas this way with him till, just in front of Mrs. Kilcannon's, who should he see, scratching himself against the wall, but Solomon, and the beast looking bitter denunciation out of the corner of his eye. Darby turned his head, ashamed to look the mistreated donkey in the face. And worse still nor that, just beyond Solomon, leaning against the same wall, was Bothered Bill Donahue, the deaf tinker. That last sight dashed Darby entirely, for he knew as well as if he had been told that the tinker was laying in wait to ride home with him for a night's lodging.

It wasn't that Darby objected on his own account to taking him home, for a tinker or a beggar-man, mind you, has a right, the world over, to claim a night's lodging and a bit to eat wherever he goes; and well, these honest people pay for it in the gossip and news they furnish at the fireside and in the good report of your family they'll spread through the country afterwards.

Darby liked well to have them come, but through some unknown weakness in her character, Bidget hated the sight of them. Worst of all, she hated Bothered Bill. She even went so far as to say that Bill was not half so bothered as he pretended— that he could hear well enough what was agreeable for him to hear, and that he was deaf only to what he didn't like to listen to.

Well, anyhow there was the tinker in the road waiting for the cart to come up, and for a while what to do Darby didn't well know.

He couldn't refuse one who asked food to eat or shelter for a wanderer's four bones during the night (that would be a sin, besides it would bring bad luck upon the house), and still he had a mortal dislike to go against Bridget in this particular— she'd surely blame him for bringing Bothered Bill home.

But at length and at last he decided, with a sigh, to put the whole case before Bill and then let him come or stay.

Whilst he was meditating on some way of conveying the news that'd be complimentary to the tinker, and that'd elevate instead of smashing that traveller's sensitiveness, Bill came up to the cart.

"The top iv the day to you, dacint man," he says. "'Tis gettin' toward dark an' I'll go home with ye for the night, I'm thinkin'," says he. The tinker, like most people who are hard of hearing, roared as though the listener was bothered.

Darby laid down the lines and held out a handful of the little medicines.

"There's nothin' the matther with me, so why should I ate thim?" cried Bill.

"They're the best thing in the worruld for that," says Darby, forcing them into Bill's mouth. "You don't know whin you'll nade thim," he says, shouting. "It's betther to meet sickness half-way," says he, "than to wait till it finds you."

And then, whilst Bill, with an open hand against his ear, was chewing the pills and looking up plaintiff into Darby's face, the knowledgeable man went on in a blandishing way to point out the situation.

"You see, 'tis this away, Wullum," he says. "It's only too daylighted I'd be to take you home with me. Indade, Bridget herself has wondherful admiraytion for you in an ord'nary way," says he. "She believes you're a raymarkable man intirely," he says, diplomatic, "only she thinks you're not clane," says he.

The tinker must have misunderstood altogether, for he bawled, in reply, "Wisha good luck to her," he says, "an' ain't I glad to have so foine opinion from so foine a woman," says he. "But sure, all the women notice how tidy I am, an' that's why they like to have me in the house. But we best be movin'," says he, coolly dropping his bags of tools into the cart, "for the night's at hand, an' a black an' stormy one it'll be," says Bill.

He put a foot onto the wheel of the cart. As he did so Darby, growing very red in the face, pressed a shilling into the tinker's hand. "Go into Mrs. Kilcannon's for the night, Wullum," he says, "an' come to us for your breakwus, an' your dinner an' maybe your supper, me good fellow," says he.

But the deaf man only pocketed the shilling and clambered up onto the seat beside Darby. "Faith, the shillin's welcome," he says; "but I'd go to such a commodious house as yours any time, Darby O'Gill, without a fardin' pay," says he, patting Darby kindly on the back. But Darby's jaw was hanging for the loss of the shilling right on top of the unwelcome visitor.

"We'd betther hurry on," says the tinker, lighting his pipe; "for afther sundown who knows what'll catch up with us on the road," says he.

Sure, there was nothing for it but to make the best of a bad bargain, and the two went on together, Darby gloomy and vexed, and the deaf man solemn but comfortable till they were almost at McHale's bridge. Then the tinker spoke up.

"Did ye hear the black threats Sheelah Maguire is makin' agin you?" he says.

"No," says Darby; "what in the worruld ails her?" says he.

"Bless the one of me knows," says the tinker, "nor anybody else for that matther. Only that last Halloween night Sheelah Maguire was bate black an' blue from head to foot, an' she lays the raysponsibility on you, Darby," he says.

The knowledgeable man had his mouth open for a question when who should go running across the road in front of them but Neddy McHale himself, and his arm full of sticks. "Go back! go back!" cries Neddy, waving an arm wild. "The bridge's butther-worruks are washed out be the flood an' McDonald's bridge is down, too, so yez must go around be the mill," says Neddy.

Now here was bitter news for you! 'Twas two miles out of the way to go by Chartres' mill, and do the best possible, they'd be passing that haunted place in the pitch dark.

"Faith, an' I've had worse luck than in pickin' you up this night, Bothered Bill Donahue," says Darby, "for it's loath I'd be to go alone—"

He turned to speak just in time, for the tinker had gathered up his bag and had put his right foot on the cart-wheel, preparing for a jump. Darby clutched the lad by the back of his neck and jolted him back hard into the seat.

"Sit still, Wullum, till we raich me own house, avourneen," he says, sarcastic, "for if ye thry that move agin I'll not lave a whole bone in your body. I'll never let it be said," he says, lofty, "that I turned one who axed me for a night's lodgin' from me door," he says. And as he spoke he wheeled the cart quick around in the road.

"Lave me down, Misther O'Gill! I think I'll stop the night with Neddy McHale," says Wullum, shivering. "Bridget don't think I'm clane," says he, as the pony started off.

"Who tould ye that, I'd like to know?" shouted Darby, growing fierce; "who dared say that of ye? You're bothered, Wullum, you know, an' so you misthrupit langwidge," he says.

But Bill only cowered down sulky, and the pony galloped down the side lane into the woods, striving to beat the rain and the darkness. But the elements were too swift-footed, and the rain came down and all the shadows met together, and the dusk whirled quick into blackness before they reached the gloomy hill.

Ever and always Chartres' mill was a misfortunate place. It broke the heart of and ruined and kilt the man who built it; and itself was a ruin these last twenty years.

Many was the wild tale known throughout the country-side of the things that had been seen and heard at that same mill, but the tale that kept Darby and the tinker unwelcome company as the pony trotted along was what had happened there a couple of years before. One night, as Paddy Carroll was driving past the gloomy old place, his best ear cocked and his weather eye open for ghosts, there came sudden from the mill three agonised shrieks for help.

Thinking 'twas the spirits that were in it, Paddy whipped up his pony and hurried on his way. But the next morning, misdoubting whether 'twasn't a human voice, after all, he had heard, Paddy gathered up a dozen of the neighbours and went back to investigate. What did they find in one of the upper rooms but a peddler, lying flat on the floor, his pack ransacked and he dead as a door-nail. 'Twas his cries Paddy had heard as the poor traveller was being murdered.

Since that time a dozen people passing the mill at night had heard the cries of the same peddler, and had seen the place blazing with lights, so, that now no one who could help it ever alone passed the mill after dark.

At the hill this side of that place the pony slowed down to a walk; neither coaxing nor beating would induce the beast to mend its steps. The horse'd stop a little and wait, and then it'd go on trembling.

They could all see the dim outlines of the empty mill glowering up at them, and the nearer they came the more it glowered, and the faster their two hearts beat. Half-way down the hill an old sign-post pointed the way with its broken arm; just beyond that the bridge, and after that the long, level road and—salvation.

But at the sign-post Clayopathra stopped dead still, staring into some bushes just beyond. She was shaking and snorting and her limbs trembling.

At the same time, to tell the truth, she was no worse off than the two Christians sitting in the cart behind her, only they were not so demonstrative about it. Small blame to the lads at that, for they were both sure and certain that lurking in the black shadows was a thing waiting to freeze their hearts with terror, and maybe to put a mark on them that they'd carry to their graves.

After coaxing Clayopathra and reasoning with her in vain, Darby, his knees knocking, turned to the tinker, and in the excitement of the events, forgetting that Bill was deaf, whispered, as cool and as easy-like as he could: "Would ye mind doin' me the favour of steppin' out, avick, an' seein' what's in that road ahead of us, Wullum?"

But Bothered Bill answered back at once, just as cool and easy: "I would mind, Darby," he says; "an' I wouldn't get down, asthore, to save you an' your family an' all their laneyal daysindents from the gallus-rope," says he.

"I thought you was deef," says Darby, growing disrespectful.

"This is no time for explaynations," says Wullum. "An' I thought meself," he went on, turning his shoulder on Darby, "that I was in company with a brave man; but I'm sorry to find that I'm riding with no betther than an' outrageous coward," says he, bitter.

Whilst Wullum was saying them vexatious words, Darby stood leaning out of the cart with a hand on Clayopathra's back and a foot on the shaft, goggling his eyes and striving to pierce the darkness at the pony's head. Without turning round he made answer: "Is that the way it is with you, Wullum?" he says, still sarcastic. "Faix, thin ye'll have that complaint no longer, for if yez don't climb down this minute, I'll trow you bag an' baggage in the ditch," he says; "so get out immaget, darlint, or I'll trow you out," says he.

The words weren't well out of his mouth when the audacious tinker whipped out his scissors and sent the sharp point half an inch into Clayopathra's flank. Clayopathra jumped, and Darby, legs and arms flying, took a back somersault that he never equalled in his supplest days, for it landed him flat against the hedge; and the leap Clayopathra gave, if she could only keep it up'd fit her for the Curragh races. And keep it up for a surprising while she did, at any rate, for as the knowlegeable man scrambled to his feet he could hear her furious gallop a hundred yards down the road.

"Stop her, Wullum avourneen, I was only joking! Come back, ye shameless rogue of the univarse, or I'll have ye thransported!" he shouted, rushing a few steps after them. But the lash of the whip on Clayopathra's sides was the only answer Wullum sent back to him.

To pursue was useless, so the deserted man slacked down to a trot. I'd hate bad to have befall me any of the hundred things Darby wished aloud then and there for Wullum.

Well, at all events, there was Darby, his head bent, plodding along through the storm, and a fiercer storm than the wind or rain ever made kept raging in his heart.

Only that through the storm in his mind there flared now and then quivers of fear and trepidation that sometimes hastened his steps and then again faltered them. Howsomever, taking it all in all, he was making good progress, and had got to the bunch of willows at the near side of the mill when one particular remembrance of Sheelah Maguire and of the banshee's comb halted the lad in the middle of the road and sent him fumbling with nervous hands in his weskit pocket. There, sure enough, was the piece of the banshee's comb. The broken bit had lain forgotten in the lad's pocket since Halloween; and now, as he felt it there next his thumping heart and buried under pipefuls of tobacco, the realisation almost floored him with consternation. All rushed over his soul like a flood.

Who else could it be but the banshee that gave Sheelah Maguire that terrible beating mentioned by the tinker? And what was that beating for, unless the banshee accused Sheelah of stealing the end of the comb? And, mother of Moses! 'Twas searching for that same bit of comb it was that brought the ghosts up from Croaghmah and made the whole townland haunted.

Was ever such a dangerous predicament! Here he was, with ghosts in the trees above him and in the hedges, and maybe looking over his shoulder, and all of them searching for the bit of enchanted comb that was in his own pocket. If they should find out where it lay what awful things they would do to him. Sure, they might call up the Costa Bower and fling him into it, and that would be the last ever heard of Darby O'Gill in the land of the living.

With them wild thoughts jumping up and down in his mind, he stood in the dark and in the rain, gawping vacant over toward the shadowy ruin. And being much agitated, the lad, without thinking, did the foolishest thing a man in his situation could well accomplish—he took out of his pocket the enchanted sliver of gold and held it to his two eyes for a look.

The consequences came sudden, for as he stuck it back into the tobacco there burst from the darkness of the willows the hollowest, most blood-curdling laugh that ever fell on mortal ears. "Ho! ho! ho!" it laughed.

The knowledgeable man's hair lifted the hat from his head.

And as if the laugh wasn't enough to scatter the wits of anyone, at the same instant it sounded, and quick as a flash, every window in the old mill blazed with a fierce blue light.

Every battered crack and crevice seemed bursting with the glare for maybe the space of ten seconds, and then, oh, millia murther! There broke from the upper floor three of the bitterest shrieks of pain and terror ever heard in this world; and, with the last cry, the mill quinched itself into darkness again and stood lonely and gloomy and silent as before. The rain pattered down on the road and the wind swished mournful in the trees, but there was no other sound.

The knowledgeable man turned to creep away very soft and quiet; but as he did, a monstrous black thing that looked like a dog without a head crawled slowly out from the willows where the terrible laugh had come from, and it crept into the gloom of the opposite hedge and there it stood, waiting for Darby to draw near.

But the knowledgeable man gave a leap backwards, and as he did, from the darkness just behind him swelled a deep sigh that was almost a groan. From the hedge to his right came another sigh, only deeper than the first, and from the blackness on his left rose another moan, and then a groaning, moaning chorus rose all round him, and lost itself in the the wailing of the wind. He was surrounded—the ghosts had captured Darby.

The lad never realised before that minute what a precious thing is daylight. If there would only come a flash of lightning to show him the faces of the surrounding spirits, horrible though they might be, he'd bid it welcome. But though the rain drizzled and the thunder rumbled, not a flare lit up the sky.

One swift, desperate hope at the last minute saved the boy from sheer despair; and that same hope was that maybe some of the Good People might be flying about and would hear him. Lifting up his face to the sky and crying out to the passing wind, he says: "Boys," he says, agonised, "lads," says he, "if there be any of yez to listen," he cried, "I'll take it as a great favour an'

I'll thank ye kindly to tell King Brian Connors that his friend an' comerade, Darby O'Gill, is in deep throuble and wants to see him imaget," says he.

"Ho! ho! ho!" laughed the terrible thing in the hedge.

In spite of the laugh he was almost sure that off in the distance a cry answered him.

To make sure he called again, but this time, though he strained his ears till their drums ached, he caught no reply.

And now, out of the murkiness in the road ahead of him, something began to grow slowly into a tall, slender, white figure. Motionless it stood, tightly wrapped in a winding sheet. In its presence a new and awful fear pressed down the heart of Darby. He felt, too, that another shade had taken its place behind him, and he didn't want to look, and strove against looking, but something forced the lad to turn his head. There, sure enough, not five feet away, stood still and silent the tall, dark figure of a man in a topcoat.

Then came from every direction low, hissing whispers that the lad couldn't understand. Something terrible would happen in a minute—he knew that well.

There's just so much fear in every man, just exactly as there is a certain amount of courage, and when the fear is all spilt a man either fights or dies. So Darby had always said.

He remembered there was a gap in the hedge nearly opposite the clump of willows, so he made up his mind that, come what might, he'd make a grand charge for it, and so into the upland meadow beyond. He waited an instant to get some strength back into his knees, and then he gave a spring. But that one spring was all he made—in that direction, at least.

For, as he neared the ditch, a dozen white, ghostly hands reached out eager for him. With a gasp he whirled in his tracks and rushed mad to the willows opposite, but there a hundred ghastly fingers were stretched out to meet the poor lad; and as he staggered back into the middle of the road again, the hero couldn't, to save his soul, keep back a long cry of terror and distress.

Immediate, from under the willows and from the ditch near the hedge and in the air above his head, from countless dead lips echoed that triumphing, unearthly laugh, Ho! ho! ho!

'Twas then Darby just nearly gave up for lost. He felt his eyes growing dim and his limbs numb. There was no air coming into his lungs, for when he tried to breathe he only gaped, so that he knew the black spell was on him, and that all that was left for him to do was to sink down in the road and then to die.

But at that minute there floated from a great way off the faint cry of a voice the despairing man knew well.

"Keep up your heart, Darby O'Gill," cried Brian Connors; "we're coming to resky you," and from over the fields a wild cheer followed them words.

"Faugh-a-balla—clear the way!" sprang the shrill war-cry of a thousand of the Good People.

At the first sound of the King's words there rose about Darby the mighty flurrying and rushing of wings in the darkness, as if tremendous birds were rising sudden and flying away, and the air emptied itself of a smothering heaviness.

So fast came the King's fairy army that the great cheer was still echoing among the trees when the gold crown of Brian Connors sparkled up from beside the knowledgeable man's knees. At that the persecuted man, sobbing with joy, knelt down in the muddy road to shake hands with his friend, the master of the Good People.

Brian Connors was not alone, for there crowded about Darby, sympathising with him, little Phelim Beg, and Nial the fiddler, and Shaun Rhue the smith, and Phadrig Oge. Also every instant, flittering out of the sky into the road, came by the score, green-cloaked and red-hooded men, following the King and ready for trouble.

"If ever a man needed a dhrop of good whisky, you're the hayro, an' this is the time an' place for it," says the King, handing up a silver-topped noggin. "Dhrink it all," he says, "an' then we'll escorch ye home. Come on," says he.

The master of the night-time turned and shouted to his subjects. "Boys," he cried, "we'll go wisible, the betther for company sake. An' do you make the 'luminaytion so Darby can see yez with him!"

At that the lovely rosy light which, as you may remember, our hero first saw in the fairy's home at Sleive-na-mon, lighted up the roadway, and under the leafy arches, bobbing along like a regiment of soldiers, all in their green cloaks and red caps, marched at least a thousand of the Little People, with Phadrig Oge at their head acting as general.

As they passed the mill five defiant pipers made the battered old windows rattle with "Garry Owen."

Part IV. The Costa Bower

So the green-dressed little army, all in the sweet, rosy light they made, went marching, to the merry music of the pipes, over the tree-bowered roadway, past the haunted brakes up the shivering hills, and down into the waiting dales, making the grim night melodious.

For a long space not a word, good, bad, or indifferent, said Darby.

But a sparrow woke her drowsy children to look at the beautiful procession, and a robin called excited to her sleepy neighbours, the linnets and the rabbits and the hares, and hundreds like them crowded delighted through the bushes, and stood peering through the glistening leaves as their well-known champions went by. A dozen venturesome young owls flew from bough to bough, following along, cracking good-natured but friendly jokes at their friends, the fairies. Then other birds came flying from miles around, twittering jubilation.

But the stern-jawed, frowny-eyed Little People for once answered back never a word, but marched stiff and silent, as soldiers should. You'd swear 'twas the Enniskillins or 'twas the Eighteenth Hussars that 'twas in it.

"Isn't that Giniral Julius Sayser at the head?" says one brown owl, flapping an audacious wing at Phadrig Oge.

"No!" cries his brother, another young villain. "'Tis only the Jook of Willington. But look at the bothered face on Darby O'Gill! Musha, are the Good People going to hang Darby?"

And faith, then, sure enough, there was mighty little elation on the features of our hero. For, as he came marching along, silent and moody, beside the King, what to do with the banshee's comb was bothering the heart out of him. If he had only thrown it to the ghosts when he was there at the mill! But that terrible laugh had crunched all sense and reason out of him, so that he forgot to do that very wise thing. Ochone, now the ghosts knew he had it; so, to throw it away'd do no good, unless they'd find it after. One thing was certain—he must some way get it back to the banshee, or else be haunted all the rest of his days.

He was sore-hearted, too, at the King, and a bit cross-tempered because the little man had stayed away so long from visiting with him.

But at last the knowledgeable man found his tongue. "Be me faix, King," he complained, "'tis a cure for sore eyes to see ye. I might have been dead an' buried an' you none the wiser," says he, sulky.

"Sure, I've been out of the counthry a fortnit," says the King, "and I've only rayturned within the hour," he says. "I wint on a suddin call to purvent a turrible war betwixt the Frinch fairies and the German fairies. I've been for two weeks on an island in the River Ryan, betwixt France an' Germany. The river is called afther an Irishman be the name of Ryan."

"At laste ye might have sint me wurrud," says Darby.

"I didn't think I'd be so long gone," says the fairy; "but the disputaytion was thraymendous," he says. The little man drew himself up dignified and scowled solemn at Darby. "They left it for me to daycide," he says, "an' this was the contintion: Fufty years ago a swan belongin' to the Frinch fairies laid a settin' of eggs on that same island, an' thin comes along a German

swan, an' what does the impident craythure do but set herself
down on the eggs laid be the Frinch swan an' hatched thim.
Afther the hatchin' the German min claimed the young ones,
but the Frinchmen pray-imp-thurribly daymanded thim back,
d'ye mind. An' the German min dayfied thim, d'ye see. So, of
course, the trouble started. For fufty years it has been growin',
an' before fightin', as a last raysort, they sint for me.

"Well, I saw at once that at the bottom of all was the ould,
ould question, which has been disthurbin' the worruld an' dhrivin'
people crazy for three thousand years."

"I know," says Darby, scornful, "'twas whither the hin that
laid the egg or the hin that hatched the egg is the mother of the
young chicken."

"An' nothin' else but that!" cried the King, surprised. "Now,
what d'ye think I daycided?" he says.

Now, your honour, I'll always blame Darby for not listening
to the King's decision, because 'tis a matter I've studied myself
considerable, and never could rightly conclude; but Darby at
the time was so bothered that he only said, in reply to the King:
"Sure, it's little I know, an' sorra little I care," he says, sulky.
"I've something more important than hin's eggs throubling me
mind, an' maybe ye can help me," he says, anxious.

"Arrah, out with it, man," says the King. "We'll find a
way, avourneen," he says, cheerful.

With that Darby up and told everything that had happened
Halloween night and since, and, indeed, by saying: "Now, here's
that broken piece of comb in me pocket, an' what to do with it I
don't know. Will ye take it to the banshee, King?" he says.

The King turned grave as a goat. "I wouldn't touch that thing in yer pocket, good friends as we are, to save yer life—not for a hundhred pounds. It might give them power over me. Yours is the only mortial hand that ever touched the banshee's comb, an' yours is the hand that should raystore it."

"Oh, my, look at that now," says Darby, in despair, nodding his head very solemn.

"Besides," says the King, without noticing him, "there's only one ghost in Croaghmah I 'ssociate with—an' that's Shaun. They are mostly oncultavated, an' I almost said raydundant. Although I'd hate to call anyone raydundant onless I had to," says the just-minded old man.

"I'll trow it here in the road an' let some of them find it," says Darby, desperate. "I'll take the chanst," says he.

"Be no manner of manes," the fairy says, "you forget that thim ghosts were once min an' women like yerself, so whin goold's consarned, they're not to be thrusted. If one should find the comb he mightn't give it to the banshee at all—he might turn 'bezzler an' 'buzzle it. No, no, you must give it to herself pursnal, or else you an' Bridget an' the childher'll be ha'nted all yer days. An' there's no time to lose, ayther," says he.

"But Bridget an' the childher's waitin' for me this minute," wailed Darby. "An' the pony, what's become of her? An' me supper?" he cried.

A little lad who was marching just ahead turned and spoke up. "The pony's tied in the stable, an' Bothered Bill has gone sneakin' off to McCloskey's," the little man says. "I saw thim as I flew past."

"Phadrig!" shouted the King. "Donnell! Conn! Nial! Phelim!" he called.

With that the little men named rose from the ranks, their cloaks spread, and come flying back like big green butterflies, and they stopped hovering in the air above Darby and the King.

"What's wanted?" asked Phelim.

"Does any of yez know where the banshee's due at this hour?" the King replied.

"She's due in County Roscommon at Castle O'Flinn, if I don't misraymimber," spoke up the little fiddler. "But I'm thinking that since Halloween she ain't worrukin' much, an' purhaps she won't lave Croaghmah."

"Well, has any one of yez seen Shaun the night, I dunno?" asked the master.

"Sorra one of me knows," says Phadrig. "Nor I," "Nor I," "Nor I," cried one after the other.

"Well, find where the banshee's stayin'," says King Brian. "An' some of yez, exceptin' Phadrig, go look for Shaun, an' tell him I want to see him purtic'lar," says the King.

The five hovering little lads vanished like a candle that's blown out.

"As for you, Phadrig," went on the master fairy, "tell the ridgiment they're to guard this townland the night, an' keep the ghosts out of it. Begin at once!" he commanded.

The words weren't well said till the whole regiment had blown itself out, and again the night closed in as black as your hat. But as it did Darby caught a glimpse from afar of the golden light of his own open door, and he thought he could see on the threshold the shadow of Bridget, with one of the children clinging to her skirt, and herself watching with a hand shading her eyes.

"Do you go home to yer supper, me poor man," says the King, "an' meantime I'll engage Shaun to guide us to the banshee. He's a great comerade of hers, an' he'll paycificate her if anyone can."

The idea of becoming acquainted personal with the ghosts, and in a friendly, pleasant way, have dealings with them, was a new sensation to Darby. "What'll I do now?" he asked.

"Go home to yer supper," says the King, "an' meet me by the withered three at Conroy's crass-roads on the sthroke of twelve. There'll be little danger to-night, I'm thinkin', but if ye should run against one of thim spalpeens, trow the bit of comb at him; maybe he'll take it to the banshee an' maybe he won't. At any rate, 'tis the best yez can do."

"Don't keep me waitin' on the crass-roads, whatever else happens," warned Darby.

"I'll do me best endayvour," says the King. "But be sure to racognise me whin I come; make no mistake, for ye'll have to spake first," he says.

They were walking along all this time, and now had come to Darby's own stile. The lad could see the heads of the children bunched up against the window-pane. The King stopped, and, laying a hand on Darby's arm, spoke up impressive: "If I come to the crass-roads as a cow with a rope about me horns ye'll lade me," he says. "If I come as a horse with a saddle on me back, yez'll ride me," says he. "But if I come as a pig with a rope tied to me lift hind leg, ye'll dhrive me," says the King.

"Oh, my! Oh, my! Oh, tare an' ages!" says Darby.

"But," says the King, waving his hand against interruptions, "so that we'll know aich other we'll have a by-worrud bechuxt us. An' it'll be poethry," he says. "So that I'll know that 'tis you that's in it, ye'll say, 'Cabbage an' bacon'; an' so that ye'll know that 'tis me that's in it, I'll answer, 'Will sthop the heart achin'.' Cabbage an' bacon will sthop the heart achin'," says the King, growing invisible. "That's good, satisfyin' poethry," he says. But the last words were sounded out of the empty air and a little way above, for the master of the night-time had vanished. At that Darby went in to his supper.

I won't expatiate to your honour on how our hero spent the evening at home, and how, after Bridget and the children were in bed, that a growing desire to meet and talk sociable with a ghost fought with twenty black fears and almost beat them. But whenever his mind hesitated, as it always did at the thought of the Costa Bower, a finger, poked into his weskit pocket where the broken bit of comb lay hid, turned the scale.

Howandever, at length and at last, just before midnight, our hero, dressed once more for the road, went splashing and plodding up the lane toward Conroy's cross-roads.

*   *   *   *   *   *   *

A man is never so brave as when sitting ferninst his own comfortable fire, a hot supper asleep in his chest, a steaming noggin of fragrant punch in his fist, and a well-tried pipe betwixt his teeth. At such times he ruminates on the old ancient heroes, and he decides they were no great shakes, after all. They had the chance to show themselves, and that's the only difference betwixt himself and themselves. But when he's flung sudden out of them pleasant circumstances, as Darby was, to go charging around in the darkness, hunting unknown and invisible dangers, much of that courage oozes out of him.

And so the strangest of all strange things was, that this night, when 'twas his fortune to be taken up by the Costa Bower, that a dread of that death-coach was present in his mind from the minute he shut the door on himself, and it outweighed all other fears.

In spite of the insurance that King Brian had given, in spite of the knowledge that his friends, the Good People, were flying hither and thither over that townland, there crept into his soul and fastened itself there the chance that the headless driver might slip past them all and gobble him up.

In vain he told himself that there were a million spots in Ireland where the death-carriage was more likely to be than in his own path. But in spite of all reasons, a dreading, shivering feeling was in his bones, so that as he splashed along he was flinging anxious looks behind or trembling at the black, wavering shadows in front.

Howsomever, there was some comfort to know that the weather was changing for the better. Strong winds had swept the worst of the storm out over the ocean, where it lingered slow, growling and sputtering lightning.

A few scattered, frowning clouds, throwing ugly looks at the moon, sulked behind.

"Lord love your shining face," says Darby, looking up to where the full moon, big as the bottom of a tub, shone bright and clear over his head. "An' it's I that hopes that the blaggard of a cloud I see creeping over at you from Sleive-na-mon won't raich you an' squinch your light before I meet up with Brian Connors."

The moon, in answer, brushed a cloud from her face, and shed a clearer, fuller light, that made the fields and dropping trees quiver and glisten.

On top of the little mound known as Conroy's Hill, and which is just this side of where the roads cross, the friend of the fairies looked about over the lonesome country-side.

Here and there gleamed a distant farm-house, a still white speck in the moonlight. Only at Con Kelley's, which was a good mile down the road, was a friendly spark of light to be seen, and that spark was so dim and so far that it only pressed down the loneliness heavier on Darby's heart.

"Wisha," says Darby, "how much I'd druther be there merry-makin' with the boys an' girls than standin' here lonesome and cowld, waiting for the divil knows what."

He strained his eyes for a sight of a horse, or a cow, or a pig, or anything that might turn out to be Brian Connors. The only thing that moved was the huge dark cloud that stretched up from Sleive-na-mon, and its heavy edge already touched the rim of the moon.

He started down the hill.

The withered tree at the cross-roads where he was to meet the King waved its blackened arms and lifted them up in warning as he came toward it, and it dripped cold tears upon his caubeen and down his neck when he stood quaking in its shadows.

"If the headless coachman were to ketch me here," he whimpered, "and fling me into his carriage, not a sowl on earth would ever know what became of me.

"I wish I wasn't so knowledgeable," he says, half crying. "I wish I was as ignorant about ghosts and fairies as little Mrs. Bradigan, who laughs at them. The more you know the more you need know. Musha, there goes the moon."

And at them words, the great blackguard cloud closed in on the moon and left the world as black as your hat.

That wasn't the worst of it by no manner of means, for at the same instant there came a rush of wind, and with it a low, hollow rumble that froze the marrow in Darby's bones. He strained his eyes toward the sound, but it was so dark he couldn't see his hand before his face.

He tried to run, but his legs turned to blocks of wood and defied him.

All the time the rumble of the terrible coach drew nearer and nearer, and he felt himself helpless as a babe. He closed his eyes to shut out the horror of the headless driver and of the poor, dead men leaning back against the seat.

At that last minute a swift hope that the King might be within hearing lent him a flash of strength, and he called out the by-word. "Cabbage an' bacon!" he cried out, despairing. "Cabbage an' bacon'll stop the heart achin'!" he roared, dismally, and then he gave a great gasp, for there was splash in the road ferninst the tree, and a tremendous black coach, with four gaunt horses and a coachman on the box, stood still as death before him.

The driver wore a brown greatcoat, the lines hung limp in his fingers, and Darby's heart stopped palpitating at the sight of the two broad, headless shoulders.

The knowledgeable man strove to cry out again, but he could only croak like a raven. "Cabbage an' bacon'll stop the heart achin'," he says.

Something moved inside the coach. "Foolish man," a voice cried, "you've not only guv the by-word, but at the same time you've shouted out its answer!"

At the voice of the King—for 'twas the King who spoke—a great weakness came over Darby, and he leaned limp against the tree.

"Suppose," the King went on, "that it was an inemy you'd met up with instead of a friend. Tare an' 'ounds! He'd have our saycret and maybe he'd put the comither on ye. Shaun," he says, up to the driver, "this is the human bean we're to take with us down to Croaghmah to meet the banshee."

From a place down on the seat on the far side of the driver a deep, slow voice, that sounded as though it had fur on it, spoke up: "I'm glad to substantiate any sarvice that will in any way conjuice to the amaylyro-ra-tion of any friend of the raynounded King Brian Connors, even though that friend be only a human bean. I was a humble human bean meself three or four hundhred years ago."

At that statement Darby out of politeness tried to look surprised.

"You must be a jook or an earl, or some other rich pillosopher, to have the most raynouned fairy in the worruld take such a shine to you," went on the head.

"Haven't ye seen enough to make yerself like him?" cried the King, raising half his body through the open window. "Didn't ye mark how ca'm an' bould he stood waitin' for ye, whin any other man in Ireland would be this time have wore his legs to the knees runnin' from ye? Where is the pillosopher except Darby O'Gill who would have guessed that 'twas meself that was in the coach, an' would have flung me the by-worrud so careless and handy?" cried the King, his face blazing with admiration.

The words put pride into the heart of our hero, and pride the world over is the twin sister of courage. And then, too, whilst the King was talking, that deep, obstreperous cloud which had covered the sky slipped off the edge of the moon and hurried to join its fellows, who were waiting for it out over the ocean. And the moon, to make amends for its late obscuration, showered down sudden a flood of such cheerful, silver light that the drooping, separate leaves and the glistening blades of grass leapt up clean and laughing to the eye. Some of that cheer went into Darby's breast, and with it crept back fresh his old confidence in his champion, the King.

But the headless driver was talking. "O'Gill," says the slow voice again, "did I hear ye say O'Gill, Brian Connors? Surely not one of the O'Gills of Ballinthubber?"

Darby answered reluctant and haughty, for he had a feeling that the monster was going to claim relationship, and the idea put a bad taste in his mouth. "All me father's people come from Ballinthubber," he says.

"Come this or come that," says the deep voice, trembling with excitement, "I'll have one look at ye." No sooner said than done; for with that saying the coachman twisted, and picking up an extraordinary big head from the seat beside him, held it up in his two hands and faced it to the road. 'Twas the face of a giant. The lad marked that its wiry red whiskers grew close under its eyes, and the flaming hair of the head curled and rolled down to where the shoulders should have been. And he saw, too, that the nose was wide and that the eyes were little. An uglier face you couldn't wish to observe.

But as he looked, the boy saw the great lips tighten and grow wide; the eyelids half closed, and the head gave a hoarse sob; the tears trickled down its nose. The head was crying.

First Darby grew uncomfortable, then he felt insulted to be cried at that way by a total stranger. And as the tears rolled faster and faster, and the sobs came louder and louder, and the ugly eyes kept leering at him affectionate, he grew hot with indignation.

Seeing which, the head spoke up, snivelling: "Plaze don't get pugnaycious nor yet disputaytious," it begged, betwixt sobs. "'Tisn't yer face that hurts me an' makes me cry. I've seen worse—a great dale worse—many's the time. But 'tis the amazin' fam'ly raysimblance that's pathrifying me heart."

The driver lifted the tail of his coat and wiped the head's two weeping eyes. "'Twas in Ballinthubber I was born an' in Ballinthubber I was rared; an' it's there I came to me misfortune through love of a purty, fair maid named Margit Ellen O'Gill. There was a song about it," he says.

"I've heerd it many an' many the time," says the King, nodding, sympathising, "though not for the last hundhred years or so." Darby glared, scornful, at the King.

"Vo! Vo! Vo!" wailed the head, "but you're like her. If it wasn't for yer bunchy red hair, an' for the big brown wen that was on her forehead, ye'd be as like as two pase."

"Arrah," says Darby, bristling, "I'm ashamed to see a man of yer sinse an' station," he says, "an' high dictation—"

"Lave off!" broke in the King, pulling Darby by the sleeve. "Come inside! Whatever else you do, rayspect the sintimintalities—they're all we have to live for, ghost or mortial," says he.

So, grumbling, Darby took a place within the coach beside his friend. He filled his pipe, and was borrowing a bit of fire from that of the King, when looking up he saw just back of the driver's seat, and opening into the carriage, a square hole of about the height and the width of your two hands. And set against the hole, staring affectionate down at him, was the head, and it smiling languishing.

"Be this an' be that," Darby growled low to the King, "if he don't take his face out of that windy, ghost or no ghost, I'll take a poke at him!"

"Be no manner of manes," says the King, anxious. "What'd we do without him? We'll be at Croaghmah in a few minutes, then he needn't bother ye."

"Why don't ye dhrive on?" says Darby, looking up surly at the head. "Why don't ye start?"

"We're goin' these last three minutes," smiled Shaun; "we're comin' up to Kilmartin churchyard now."

"Have you passed Tom Grogan's public-house?" asked the King, starting up, anxious.

"I have, but I can turn back agin," says the face, lighting up, interested.

"They keep the best whisky there in this part of Ireland," says the King. "Would ye mind steppin' in an' bringing us out a sup, Darby agra?"

Mistress Tom Grogan was a tall, irritated woman, with sharp corners all over her, and a temper that was like an east wind. She was standing at her own door, argufying with Garge McGibney and Wullum Broderick, and dealing them out hard names, whilst her husband, Tom, a mild little man, stood within, leaning on the bar, smoking sedately. Garge and Wullum were argufying back at Mistress Grogan, telling her what a fine-looking, respectable woman she was, and couldn't they have one drop more before going home, when they saw coming sliding along through the air toward them, about four feet above the ground, a decent-dressed man, sitting comfortable, his pipe in his mouth and one leg crossed over the other. The stranger stopped in the air not five feet away, and in the moonlight they saw him plain knock the ashes from his pipe and stick it in the rim of his caubeen.

They caught hold of each other, gasping as he stepped down out of the air to the ground, and wishing them the top of the evening, he brushed past, walked bold to the bar and briskly called for three jorums of whisky. Tom, oblivious—for he hadn't seen—handed out the drinks, and the stranger, natural as you please, emptied one, wiped his mouth with the back of his hand and started for the door, carrying the two other jorums.

Tom, of course, followed out to see who was in the road, and then he clutched hold of the three others, and the four, gripping each other like lobsters boiling in the pot, clung, speechless, swaying back and forth.

And sure 'twas no wonder, for they saw the strange man lift the two cups in the naked air, and they saw plain the two jorums leave his hands, tip themselves slowly over until the bottoms were uppermost—not one drop of the liquor spilling to the ground. They saw no more, for they each gave a different kind of roar when Darby turned to bring back the empty vessels. The next second Tom Grogan was flying like a hunted rabbit over the muddy petatie-field behind his own stable, whilst Wullum Broderick and Garge McGibney were dashing furious after him like Skibberbeg hounds. But Mrs. Grogan didn't run away, because she was on her own threshold, lying on the flat of her back, and for the first time in her life, speechless.

Howandever, with a rumble and a roar, the coach with its travellers went on its way.

The good liquor supplied all which that last sight lacked that was needful to put our three heroes in good humor with themselves and with each other, so that it wasn't long before their troubles, being forgot, they were conversing sociable and familiar, one with the other.

Darby, to improve his information, was striving to make the best of the situation by asking knowledgeable questions. "What kind of disposition has the banshee, I dunno?" he says, after a time.

"A foine creachure, an' very rayfined, only a bit too fond of crying an' wailing," says Shaun.

"Musha, I know several livin' women that cap fits," says the knowledgeable man. "Sure, does she do nothin' but wail death keens? Has she no good love-ballads or songs like that? I'd think she'd grow tired," he says.

"Arrah, don't be talkin'!" says Shaun. "'Tis she who can sing them. She has one in purticular—the ballad of 'Mary McGinnis'—that I wisht ye could hear her at," he says.

"The song has three splendid chunes to it, an' the chune changes at aich varse. I wisht I had it all, but I'll sing yez what I have," he says. With that the head began to sing, and a fine, deep singing voice it had, too, only maybe a little too roaring for love-ballads:

"Come all ye thrue lovers, where'er yez may be,
 Likewise ye desayvers be land or be sea;
 I hope that ye'll listen with pity to me
 Since the jew'l of me life is a thraitor."

"Here's where the chune changes," says the head, licking his lips.

"On goin' to church last Sunday me thrue love
    passed me by,
 I knew her mind was changed be the twinklin' of
    her eye;
 I knew her mind was changed, which caused me for
    to moan,
 'Tis a terrible black misfortin to think she cowld has
    grown."

"That's what I call rale poethry," says Darby.

"There's no foiner," says the King, standing up on the seat, his face beaming.

"The next varse'll make yez cry salt tears," says Shaun. And he sang very affecting:

"Oh, dig me a grave both large, wide, an' deep,
An' lay me down gently, to take me long sleep;
Put a stone at me head an' a stone at me feet,
Since I cannot get Mary McGinnis."

"Faith, 'tis a foine, pittiful song," says Darby, "an' I'd give a great dale if I only had it," says he.

"Musha, who knows; maybe ye can get it," says the old King with a wink. "Ye may daymand the favour of the three wishes for bringing her what yer bringin'," he whispered. "Shaun!" he says, out loud, "do ye think the banshee'll give that song for the bringing back of the lost comb, I dunno?"

"I dunno meself," says the head, dubious.

"Bekase if she would, here's the man who has the comb, an' he's bringin' it back to her."

The head gave a start and its eyes bulged with gladness. "Then it's the lucky man I am entirely," he says. "For she promised to stick me head on and to let me wear it purmanent, if I'd only bring tidings of the comb," says Shaun. "She's been in a bad way since she lost it. You know the crachure can sing only whin she's combing her hair. Since the comb's broke her woice is cracked scand'lous, an' she's bitther ashamed, so she is. But here's Croaghmah right before us. Will yez go in an' take a dhrop of something?" says he.

Sticking out his head, Darby saw towering up in the night's gloom, bleak Croaghmah, the mountain of the ghosts; and, as he thought of the thousands of shivering things inside, and of the unpleasant feelings they'd given him at Chartres' mill a few hours before, a doubt came into his mind as to whether it were best to trust himself inside. He might never come out.

Howandever, the King spoke up, saying, "Thank ye kindly, Shaun, but ye know well that yerself an' one or two others are the only ghosts I 'ssociate with, so we'll just step out, an' do you go in yerself an' tell the banshee we're waitin'. Rayturn with her, Shaun, for ye must take Darby back."

With that the two heroes descended from the coach, and glad enough was Darby to put his brogues safe and sound on the road again.

All at once the side of the mountain ferninst them opened with a great crash, and Shaun, with the coach and horses, disappeared in a rush, and were swallowed up by the mountain, which closed after them. Darby was blinking and shivering beside the King, when sudden, and without a sound, the banshee stood before them.

She was all in white, and her yellow hair strealed to the ground. The weight and sorrow of ages were on her pale face.

"Is that you, Brian Connors?" she says. "An' is that one with you the man who grabbled me?"

"Your most obadient," says the King, bowing low; "it was an accident," says he.

"Well, accident or no accident," she says severe, "'tis the foine lot of throuble he's caused me, an' 'tis the illigant lot of throuble he'd a had this night if you hadn't saved him," she says. The banshee spoke in a hollow voice, which once in a while'd break into a squeak.

"Let bygones be bygones, ma'am, if you plaze," says Darby, "an' I've brought back yer comb, an' by your lave I ax the favour of three wishes," says he.

Some way or other he wasn't so afeared now that the King was near, and besides, one square, cool look at any kind of trouble—even if 'tis a ghost—takes half the dread from it.

"I have only two favours to grant any mortial man," says she, "an' here they are." With that she handed Darby two small black stones with things carved on them. "The first stone'll make you onwisible if you rub the front of it, an' 'twill make you wisible again if you rub the back of it. Put the other stone in yer mouth an' ye can mount an' ride the wind. So Shaun needn't dhrive yez back," she says.

The King's face beamed with joy.

"Oh, be the hokey, Darby me lad," says he, "think of the larks we'll have thravellin' nights together over Ireland ground, an' maybe we'll go across the say," he says.

"But fairies can't cross runnin' water," says Darby, wondering.

"That's all shuperstition," says the King. "Didn't I cross the river Ryan? But, ma'am," says he, "you have a third favour, an' one I'm wishin' for mightily meself, an' that is, that ye'll taiche us the ballad of 'Mary McGinnis.'"

The banshee blushed. "I have a cowld," says she.

"'Tis the way with singers," says the King, winking at Darby, "but we'll thank ye to do yer best, ma'am," says he.

Well, the banshee took out her comb, and fastening to it the broken end, she passed it through her hair a few times and began the song.

At first her voice was pretty weak and trembling, but the more she combed the stronger it grew, till at last it rose high and clear, and sweet and wild as Darby'd heard it that Halloween night up at McCarthy's.

The two heroes stood in the shadow of a tree, Darby listening and the King busy writing down the song. At the last word the place where she had been standing flashed empty and Darby never saw her again.

I wisht I had all the song to let your honour hear it, and maybe I'll learn it from Darby by the next time ye come this way. And I wisht I had time to tell your honour how Darby, one day having made himself invisible, lost the stone, and how Bothered Bill Donahue found it, and how Bill, rubbing it by accident, made *himself* invisible, and of the terrible time Darby had a-finding him.

But here's Kilcuny, and there's the inn, and—thank ye! God bless your honour!

THE END